THE COGGLY POON

Written and Illustrated by David Hornsby

Contents

GRANDPA WITH A GOLF CLUB

My portrait is a likeness
Quite astounding to behold…
Yet Dominic, the artist,
Is only five years old!
How truly he has captured
My blank bewildered stare,
My shapeless figure, stumpy legs
And little tuffs of hair!
It's hardly very flattering
But then, why should it be?
For everyone who sees it
Knows at once that it is me!

SUSIE THE SNAKE

There was a snake called Susie
Who'd forgotten how to hiss!
She tried so hard to do so,
But all she said was this:

"I am a thnake called Thoothie,
I've forgotten how to hith!
I try tho hard to do tho,
But all I thay ith THITHHHHH!

LACK OF INFORMATION

If only I knew which and who
I'd pass the answer on to you.
If only I knew how and why
I'd be delighted to reply.
If only I knew when and where
Then I would tell you then and there.
But sadly, here at Euston Station,
We're rather short of information!

YOU NEVER KNOW
(A poem of six words)

Do you think I never know you?
I know you think you never do!
You think you do? I never know...
I never think, you know!   Do you?

TOM'S BOMB

There was a boy whose name was Tom
Who made a high-explosive bomb,
By mixing up some plasticine
With sugar, flour and margarine,
And also (tho' the smell was queer)
A drop of Father's home-made beer!
He took it off to school one day,
And when they all went out to play
He left it by the radiator...
But as the heat was getting greater
The mixture in the bomb grew thick,
And very soon it seemed to tick!
Miss Knight came in and gazed with awe
To see the bomb upon the floor.
"Dear me!" she said, "It is a bomb!
An object worth escaping from!"
She went to Mr. Holliday
And said to him in some dismay:
"Headmaster, this is not much fun!
There is a bomb in Classroom One!"
"Great snakes!" said he, and gave a cough,
"You don't suppose it might go off?
But on the off-chance that it does
I think we'd better call the fuzz!"

A policeman came, and said "Oh God!
We need the bomb-disposal squad...
A doctor and some firemen too,
A helicopter and its crew,
And since I'm shaking in the legs
A pot of tea and hard-boiled eggs!"
A bomb-disposal engineer
Said with every sign of fear,

"I've not seen one like that before!"
And rushed out screaming through the door!
Everyone became more worried,
Till Tom, who seemed to be unflurried,
Said "What is all the fuss about?
I'll pick it up and take it out!"
He tipped the contents down the drain
And peace and quiet reigned again!
Tom just smiled and shook his head
And quietly to himself he said:
"Excitement's what these people seek...
I'll bring another one next week!"

MISS CHINN

Miss Chinn was always cheerful,
You never saw her frown.
She was exasperating
For you couldn't get her down!
At last she made me so annoyed
A dreadful thing occurred:
I went and called her 'Fishface'!
And I knew she must have heard!

Next day, in shame, I said to her,
"I must apologise
For saying 'Fishface' yesterday..."
But then, to my surprise,
She smiled her irritating smile
And said, "I'm glad you did!
I backed Fishface in the Derby
And won nearly twenty quid!"

GLOP

Do you find that life is stressful?
Do you sometimes feel a flop?
What you need, to be successful,
Is a tin of magic GLOP!

GLOP's amazing! GLOP's fantastic!
For every purpose, GLOP's a must!
GLOP mends china, glass and plastic,
And protects your car from rust!

GLOP makes coughs and sneezes vanish...
Simply rub it on your chest!
And, moreover, GLOP will banish
Every sort of garden pest!

Balding men will find that GLOP'll
Stop their hair from falling out!
And the very smallest drop'll
Cure the toothache or the gout!

Soothing GLOP is so propitious
For sensitive or itchy skins!
GLOP on toast is quite delicious
And it's full of vitamins!

GLOP will shine your chairs and tables,
GLOP will stop you snoring...and
Those who save the special labels
Could win a trip to Disneyland!

GLOP will stop your shoes from squeaking,
GLOP will shift those stubborn stains,
GLOP will stop your roof from leaking,
Keep you slim, and clear the drains!

Now I'm sure you'll want to try it,
So, it gives me great regret
To tell you that you cannot buy it:
It hasn't been invented yet!

I'D HATE TO BE...

I'd hate to be a pillar-box...
There's nothing you could do
When people saw your open mouth
And shoved their letters through!
I'd hate it when the postman
Came cycling down the lane,
For he'd unlock my poor old tum
And take them out again!

I'd hate to be a wooden spoon...
Imagine if you found
You were plunged into a pan of soup
And slowly stirred around!
How hot and sticky it would be!
Your only hope, it's plain,
Would be to hide in the kitchen drawer,
Never to stir again!

I'd hate to be a tennis ball...
How battered you would get
When tennis players whacked you
To and fro across the net!
And then, when you were old and grey,
You know what they would do?
They'd give you to the dog and say:
"Here Rover! Have a chew!

HOW TO WRITE POETRY

Writing poetry, my dears,
Is not as hard as it appears!
The secret I will now reveal:
SIT DOWN AND EAT A HEARTY MEAL!
For inspiration seldom comes
To poets who have empty tums!
If first you feed the inner man
Your rhymes will flow, your verses scan.
The famous poets knew this well
As my researches plainly tell:

Lord Tennyson ate venison,
And Coleridge liked a roast...
But Keats confessed he wrote his best
When eating buttered toast!

Will Shakespeare knew that Irish stew
Would help him write a sonnet,
And Wordsworth said he liked brown bread
With peanut butter on it!

"A ploughman's lunch is good to munch!"
So Thomas Gray maintained,
And when Milton had some Stilton
He wrote Paradise Regained"!

Thomas Hood liked Yorkshire pud,
Lord Byron ate sardines,
On pumpkin pie did Pope rely
But Burns liked curried beans!

"A juicy steak," said William Blake,
Makes inspiration come!"
"Til fish and chips have passed my lips,"
  Said Shelley, "I am dumb!"

Rupert Brooke would ask his cook,
For puddings stuffed with dates
"I owe my art to treacle tart!"
Said William Butler Yeats!

So now you know! Just bear in mind
That when the rhymes are hard to find
That empty feeling makes it harder:
Lay down your pen and raid the larder!
I had a three-course lunch today...
And lo! I felt without delay
A surge of great creative power:
I wrote all this in half an hour!
I'm going to have my tea at four...
And then I'll write a whole lot more!

RADIO PHONE-IN

"Time for one more call before
The weather and the news,
So hallo Dave in Doncaster!
We'd like to hear your views!"

"Hallo? It's like...Well, fair enough,
I mean, but like I say
It's kind of you know sort of thing...
Know what I mean, OK?"

THE FRENCH CAT

A cat I met
In Gay Paree
Could count in French
From one to three!
I said to him:
Excusez-moi,
But what comes after
UN
DEUX
TROIS?
Miaow! Miaow!, the QUATRE
Plied. My spirits CINQ,
He would not SIX!
Then he up- SEPT
My shredded HUIT
And said, I've had a NEUF
Of DIX!

THE GIZMO

I used to have a gizmo
But the whatsit was too big,
So I gave the whole caboodle
To Mrs. Thingummyjig.
She said, "There's no what-have-you
And where's the doodah gone?
It would cause a how's-your-father
If I switched the thingy on!"

OUR FRIENDS THE ANIMALS

The anaconda, bless his soul,
Likes to swallow people whole...
-And that is why my Auntie Joyce
Talks in that rather muffled voice.

The big brown bear is full of charms,
He loves to hug you in his arms...
-And that is why my cousin Beth
Is feeling rather out of breath.

The giant gorilla gives a bound
And grabs your hand and swings you round..
-And that is why my little brother
Has one arm longer than the other.

The ostrich eats what he can find.
If meals are odd, he doesn't mind!
-And that explains why Uncle Matt
Is now without his bowler hat.

The golden eagle roams the skies...
He swoops! He grabs! And off he flies!
-And that explains why Baby Clare
Has gone for a breath of mountain air!

The patient tiger smiles and waits...
His dinner he anticipates!
And that's the simple reason we
Are sitting in this blooming tree!

THE COGGLY POON

(All the words in this poem can be found in
the dictionary)

Among the swaying talipots
Beside the blue lagoon,
On the fringes of the jungle
There stood a coggly poon.

The coggly poon was very tall,
Though still not fully grown,
And in its topmost branches lived
A hoolock, all alone.

How happy was the hoolock
In this delightful spot!
What if the poon was coggly?
To him it mattered not!

Never was he lonely,
For among the birds he knew
Were a grackle and a butterbump,
To mention only two.

And so, the hoolock lived in peace
Until one afternoon
A fizgig with two friends came by
And saw the coggly poon!

The fizgig grew excited
And told her friends to stop.
"Let's climb this coggly poon," she cried,
"Until we reach the top!"

But sensibly her friends preferred
To swim in the lagoon.
"Only a liripoop," they said,
"Would climb a coggly poon!"

And so, the fizgig climbed alone,
Against her friends' advice.
"You doddypolls!" she yelled at them,
Which wasn't very nice!

The coggly poon was gliddery,
And difficult to climb,
For wimble as the fizgig was
It coggled all the time.

The hoolock saw her climbing up,
And very grumly said:
"I wish she'd climb a groo-groo
Or a hackmatack instead!"

Then angrily he leapt about,
And such was his endeavour,
That very soon the coggly poon
Was cogglier than ever!

From side to side the hoolock leapt,
And up and down as well...
He shook that coggly poon so hard
The fizgig slipped and fell!

Down and down the fizgig fell
And landed on her head!
Her friends came running up to help:
"You jobernowl!" they said.

With water from a goglet
They bathed her face and feet...
They gave her persico to drink
And popperings to eat.

But oh! the pain was grooly
As on the ground she lay,
So, they put her on a doolie
And they carried her away.

The grackle and the butterbump
Declared it served her right,
And the hoolock smiled a simian smile
Of triumph and delight!

And no-one since has ever dared
To climb that coggly poon,
Among the swaying talipots,
Beside the blue lagoon!

PRETTY ELSIE

When Eddie offered Elsie
A cheese and onion crisp,
Neither of them was aware
The other had a lisp!
He said, "You're pretty, Elthie!"
But she answered pretty quick:
"You may think I'm pretty 'ealthy,
But I'm really pretty thick!"

THE DENTIST AND THE CROCODILE

A crocodile with toothache
Is a miserable beast,
For dentists who treat crocodiles
Are rare, to say the least.
This is because the crocodile,
When asked to 'open wide'
May feel a trifle peckish
When the dentist peers inside.
The dentist says: "This will not hurt,
So just keep still, old chap!"
And suddenly the massive jaws
Close with a vicious snap.
The crocodile sheds many tears
And feels extremely sad,
For there's no sign of the dentist
And his toothache's just as bad!

THE ANSWER SHOP

Near the foot of Primrose Hill,
Where all the buses stop,
Lived old Professor Fothergill,
Who ran The Answer Shop.

Whatever people wished to know,
He told them for a penny.
He was infallible, and so
His customers were many!

He knew the Patron Saint of Wales,
The date of Waterloo,
The proper way of cooking snails,
And why the sky is blue,

The name of Doctor Johnson's cat,
The cure for indigestion...
He always had the answer pat
To every single question!

No-one caught him out until
One sunny day in spring
I asked Professor Fothergill:
How long is a piece of string?

The old Professor scratched his head
And started muttering...
I'm sure I ought to know, he said,
The length of a piece of string!

He hunted through 'The Book of String',
And sighed aloud, because
It told him every single thing
Except how long it was!

Poor Professor Fothergill
Was stumped, without a doubt!
He's looking for the answer still
But cannot find it out!

There is an answer, I suppose...
It's such a simple thing!
There must be somebody who knows
The length of a piece of string!

MISS CHOLMONDELEY

Miss Cholmondeley ran o'er hill and dale
Down to the moonlit lake...
She sang like Florence Nightingale
And swam like Francis Drake!

She danced 'til break of Doris Day
Along the Bernard Shaw...
How Oscar Wilde if she could stay
For ever Henry Moore!

But by the babbling Rupert Brooke
Her hunger did awaken...
So off she ran to Captain Cook
An egg with Francis Bacon.

HUSH-A-BYE

Baby wouldn't sleep until
We placed him on the window sill...
We knew his cries would shortly cease...
He soon dropped off and all was peace!

THE JURY

The members of the jury
Spent a long and anxious time
Deciding if the prisoner
Was guilty of the crime.

The foreman of the jury
(Let us call him Mr. A)
Addressed his fellow members
In a most impressive way:

'Let justice now be done,' he said,
By twelve good men and true...'
At that, six ladies shouted 'Hey!
We're on the jury too!'

'The question is,' said Mr. A,
'Did Albert Blenkinsopp
Purloin a tin of butter beans
From Bingley's corner shop?

We've heard the evidence in court,
So, let us now agree...
Is he innocent or guilty?
How say you, Mr. B?'

'The evidence,' said Mr. B,
'Escaped me, I'm afraid...
I came to court this morning
Without my hearing aid!'

'I think he's guilty!' cried Miss C,
I've known it all along!
His eyes were shifty, and besides
His hair was far too long!'

'I must agree,' said Mr. D,
'It may sound rather harsh,
But surely no-one but a thief
Could wear that foul moustache!'

'He's innocent!' said Mr. E,
'I vote we let him go!
He swore he wasn't guilty
And he surely ought to know!'

'I'm sure he didn't do it!'
Mrs. F began...
'But if he did,' she added,
'He's a very naughty man!'

Miss G said it was wrong to steal
A tin of butter beans...
It would have been far healthier
To steal some tangerines!

'The problem is,' said Mrs. H,
'My concentration's gone!
All morning I've been worried
That I left the cooker on!'

'Now wait a bit,' said Mr. I,
'A thought occurs to me!
Suppose we ring that little bell
And ask them for some tea!'

'A good idea!' said Mr. J,
'I'm dying for a cup!
And then let's vote him guilty
And wrap the whole thing up!'

'You heartless man!' cried Mrs. K,
'Suppose he's got a cat!
If he's sent away to prison,
Who would feed it? Tell me that!'

'Well, don't ask me!' said Mrs. L,
'I've really no idea!
The only thing I do know is
We're paid for sitting here!'

Then finally the foreman spoke:
'Let's toss a coin!' said he,
'Heads he's guilty, tails he's not!
That seems quite fair to me!'

The verdict was unanimous...
They all agreed: 'It's tails!'
So, Albert Blenkinsopp is free...
And justice still prevails!

THE LINGUIST

"Ja!" said Heinrik, "I can speak
Four languages as well as Dutch!
I'm here already since one week,
London I like extremely much!"

"You speak five languages?" said Joe,
"Cor! I can only manage one!
Your English aint 'alf funny, though...
You don't talk proper, my old son!"

BEETHOVEN, BEETHOVEN

Beethoven, Beethoven,
Mozart and Strauss…
We've a musical dog
In our musical house!
He listens to Schubert
And Bach and Ravel,
Rossini, Puccini,
Vivaldi as well.
He growls at Stravinsky
And bristles at Liszt,
But Brahms and Debussy
He cannot resist!
By Handel and Haydn
The dog is obsessed,
But Beethoven, Beethoven pleases him best!

THE SPACE ROCKET

10..... The count-down has begun!

9...... I'm counting down to one!

8...... I'm off to outer space!

7...... Goodbye rocket base!

6...... The boosters start to roar!

5...... I hope they've shut the door!

4...... Control, we're looking good!

3...... All systems GO (touch wood!).

2...... We'll lift-off in a tick!!

1...... Oh help! I'm feeling sick!

ZERO...That's enough for me...

Mission cancelled! Time for tea!

MY GOATS

Margery is small and gentle,
Billy's very fierce and large,
So, when I'm butted from behind
I know the butter isn't Marge!

JAMES' GRANDFATHER

"Come and meet my grandfather!"
Suggested James one day,
"I'm sure that you would like him!"
So, I replied "O.K.!"

"You'll find," said James, "he's very old,
Though tall and handsome still,
So, you must show him great respect!"
I said "Of course I will!"

"I'm very pleased to meet you, Sir!"
I said. But what a shock!
He only answered "Whirr-ker-chunk!"
And then chimed six o'clock!

SONG OF A MADMAN

I'm singing in the rain,
Just singing in the rain!
I've a curious feeling
I'm going insane!
I dance through the town
With a lunatic grin…
It's bucketing down
And I'm soaked to the skin!
I'm singing in the rain,
Just singing in the rain!
Now I am peeling
My clothes off again!
I've water on the brain
And that would explain
Why I'm singing
And dancing
In the rain!

THE SUPER-ATHLETE

James can run
Faster than a cheetah!
James can jump
Like a kangaroo!
James is as strong
As a giant gorilla!
James can swim
Like a dolphin too!
This means James
Will take some beating
Whenever they hold
The Olympic Games!
So there's not much point
In the others competing...
For ALL the Gold Medals
Will be won by James!

AT THE CHECK-OUT

With patience on the whole I queue
Behind a dear old soul like you,
For one day I may grow like you
And be confused and slow like you
And told I have a low IQ...
And so I smile although I queue
Behind a dear old soul like you
Who's clearly lost control like you!

THE THIN QUEEN

(Anne Boleyn, second wife of Henry the Eighth was
extremely thin and 'rather flat-chested')

King Henry said
To Anne Boleyn:
My dear, we think you're
Far too theyn!
You're scarcely fatter
Than a peyn!
Your shape is most
Unfemineyn!
An appetite
Is not a seyn...
So, copy us...
Start tucking eyn!
You too can have
A double cheyn!
Be fat and happy,
Anne Boleyn!

....

Thus Henry spoke,
But Anne Boleyn
Remained, alas,
All bones and skeyn:
King Henry simply
Could not weyn!

ON BLEDON HILL

On BLEDON HILL lives Mr. McGill,
Which makes him feel surprised...
He used to live on WIMBLEDON HILL...
But the sign was vandalized!

THE COCKATOO

One winter's day, while strolling through
The aviary at London Zough,
I saw a handsome cockatough
Perched high upon a tall bambough.
He looked at me and down he flough
And said, "I'd like a word with yough!"
I was surprised, for hithertough
I'd never met a cockatough
Who talked. I said, "How do you dough?"
And then, as my amazement grough,
He said, "It's boring in the Zough!
There's hardly anything to dough
And no-one here worth talking tough…
The parrots are a motley crough
Who mostly haven't got a clough!
Oh, I amuse myself, it's trough,
By calling 'Cock-a-doodle-dough!'
To fool the people passing through...
They're idiots...apart from yough!"

So, then I asked the cockatough,
"Supposing you could leave the Zough,
Where would you go, what would you
 dough?"
"I'd fly," he said, "to Timbuktough!
Or Florida! Or Khatmandhough!
To where the skies are always blough!
And then I'd spend a week or twough
With my relations in Perough!
Ah, well," remarked the cockatough,
"It's closing time, so toodle-ough!"
So, saying, without more adough,
He spread his wings and up he flough
To perch upon the tall bambough.

And as I turned to leave the Zough,
I heard him hoot: "Tu-whit-tu-whough!"

Since then, whenever I feel blough,
I take the train to Waterlough,
And then the tube to London Zough,
To see my friend, the cockatough!

ELIZA BICKERSTAFF

I gave Eliza Bickerstaff

The works of Shelley, bound in calf,

To show my deep devotion.

And oh! the easy grace with which

She tossed the volume in the ditch...

T'was poetry in motion!

INDIGESTION

Never hurry over curry...
Eat your ravioli slowly!
If you are a greedy gobbly
Your tummy will be wobbly prob'ly.

PEGGY BABCOCK

It is hard to say your name,
Peggy Babpock!
Isn't it a shame,
Pebby Bagpock!
But you are not to blame,
Becky Bogcap,
And I love you just the same,
Baggy Peckbob!

ALBERT PYM

Albert Pym was getting dressed.
He donned his pants, and then his vest...
When suddenly his wife said, "Bert!
Here you are: a clean white shirt!
You know I like you to look smart,
So, put it on, my dearest heart!"
"Thank you, my dear!" said Mr. Pym.
(She always took such care of him!)

So, Mrs. Pym sat on the bed
And watched, as Albert thrust his head,
And then his arms and shoulders too
Into the shirt, as people do.
But this was not his lucky day,
For Albert found to his dismay
That something odd was going on:
The opening for his head was gone!
And then he thought, "How very weird!
The armholes too have disappeared!"
He lurched and struggled round the floor
And banged his elbow on the door,
Experiencing, stage by stage,
Annoyance, bafflement and rage!
For several minutes, Mrs. Pym
Just giggled as she looked at him,
For Mr. Pym, encased in white,
Was certainly a comic sight,
And very soon his muffled cries
Brought tears of laughter to her eyes.
"Oh, Bert," she spluttered through her tears,
"I haven't laughed so much for years!"
...At last there came a frantic shout:
"Help! Help! I'm stuck, I can't get out!"
"Enough's enough," thought Mrs. Pym,
I really must enlighten him!"
She shouted, "Can you hear me, Bert?
That thing you're wearing's not a shirt!
I cannot wait to see your face
When you remove that pillow-case!
You ought to know by now, my dear,
I 'April-Fool' you every year!"

EAVESDROPPING

I sat behind two ladies
On the bus to Brighton Pier
And I didn't men to listen
But I couldn't help but hear:

So anyway we had our tea
And then I said to Syd,
You promised you would get me one
And then you never did!

It isn't much to ask, I said…
(He saw I was upset)
Calm down, he said, I'll get you one!
I said, Well, don't forget!

So in the evening in he comes
And shows me what he'd got.
He said, I hope you're satisfied!
I told him: No I'm not!

So then he said, What's wrong with it?
I said, It's far too small!
Unless I have a bigger one
I don't want one at all!

Just look at it, I said to him.
I can't believe my eyes!
That Mrs. Jones has got one
And hers is twice the size!"

But then they both got off the bus
And my thoughts went out to Syd...
I hope he got a bigger one...
I wonder if he did?

WHAT FARMERS SAY

When sheep do gather close together
There will be cold and windy weather.
When cows do stand up hindlegs first
You should anticipate the worst.
When horses lie down on the grass
A thunderstorm will come to pass.
When goats are bleating night and day
It means that rain is here to stay.
But farmers say: When pigs can fly
The weather will be fine and dry!

LETTER FROM AN UNCLE

Dear Tom, How pleasant to receive
Your interesting letter.
At last I really do believe
Your spelling's getting better!
But one thing made me scratch my head
In growing consternation:
Your letter showed a total lack
Of any punctuation!
I read it in bewilderment,
And breathlessly, because
You wrote from start to finish
Without a single pause!
And so I'm sending you this book
Which will, I hope, explain
The subject clearly. Study it
Before you write again!
I hope, therefore, that when you do
I shall not gasp for breath!
Affectionately, Uncle Bill,
(And love from Auntie Eth).

REPLY FROM HIS NEPHEW

Dear Uncle comma paragraph
You are extremely kind
Full stop the book is great and I
Am very underlined
Pleased full stop I never grasped
This punctuation lark
Until I read it colon thank
You exclamation mark

Bracket as I turned each page
I could not help but laugh
Hilariously dot dot dot
Close bracket paragraph
And how is Auntie question mark
I hear that she has started
A home for hamsters dash my aunt
Is tender hyphen hearted
Full stop how nice it is to know
You will not blow your top
To read this letter comma lots
Of love from Tom full stop

JEMIMA JONES

Jemima Jones was pale and thin,
With spindly legs and flawless skin.
Six feet tall with orange hair,
She wore a supercilious air
And reckoned it would be a doddle
To tread the catwalks as a model.
But soon, forsaking lunch and dinner,
The foolish girl grew even thinner.
Now human beings, by convention,
Require to have a third dimension…
So pity poor Jemima who
Reduced herself to only two!
This of course was bound to mean
That sideways she could not be seen.
Inevitably after that
Jemima's life was rather flat.

POGGLA'S QUILLIES

Poggla, snoozling in her zizzla,
(In her chimey pampaloomas),
Was a-goggle for some quillies
So, she klonged the dongle-ding!
"Gosper! Gosper!" yackled Poggla,
"Bring my quillies, huppy-huppy!
Lots of scrumbly-gumbly quillies!
Spikky-spiff, you bonderling!"

Ulgently, the lumless Gosper
Troddled into Poggla's zizzla,
With a kipkinful of quillies,
Chuzzling on a moolibar.
"Huppy-huppy!" grumpled Poggla,
"Are my quillies licksy-dicksy?
Are they really scrumbly-gumbly?"
And Gosper sookled: "Yes, they are!"

Then, OOPSI-BUSKINS! He unscootled
All the scrumbly-gumbly quillies
Over Poggla's pampaloomas,
Down her twinky doodle-dah!
CRIMPO! How the quillies chuzzled!
But Gosper, with a waley cruckle,
Troddled from the zizzla, croodling:
"Scrumbly-gumbly! Har-har-har!"

(Note: For best results, quillies should
be lightly flumed and served with a
squidge of doff.)

WOE! WOE!

"Woe! Woe! Woe the boat

Gently down the stweam!

Mewwily, mewwily, mewwily, mewwily,

Life is but a dweam!"

When little children sing this song

How painful does it seem!

I'm not a squeamish person but...

They make me want to squeam!

THE UNDERTAKER

The undertaker undertakes
To drive the hearse extremely slowly...
Not for him the squeal of brakes
Or travel at a speed unholy!
So copy him for heaven's sake
Unless you want to meet your maker,
And never ever undertake
To overtake an undertaker!

THE LITTLE WIBLEY HARVEST FEAST

Colonel Drury is the man
Who every year is asked to plan
The Harvest Feast they always hold
At Little Wibley–on-the-Wold.
"Leave it to me," the Colonel said,
"The secret is to plan ahead.
You need a clever chap you know
To organize this sort of show…
A chap who's always going to be
Calm and in control, like me!"

And so as always, on the night
The Village Hall was quite a sight
With fruit and vegetables and flowers…
(Arranging them had taken hours).
A sumptuous banquet had been planned
With music by the Village Band
And even more exciting yet,
High up above there was a net
With large balloons, to be released
At the conclusion of the Feast!

.The Colonel chuckled with delight
And said, "We'll have some fun tonight!
The evening's bound to swing along!"
Unfortunately, he was wrong!
A hundred villagers at least
Had gathered for the Village Feast…
Expectancy was in the air
With happy faces everywhere.
But little Lucy Brown was glum
And said she wished she hadn't come…
She told her mother she was sure
The Harvest Feast would be a bore!

It might have been If Elsie Toop
Had not been asked to serve the soup.
A highly nervous woman who
Would faint if anyone said "Boo!"
She carried an enormous pot
Of onion soup, all piping hot,
And Lucy, standing right beside her,
Said "Boo!" and waved her plastic spider!

Well, Elsie fainted then and there…
The steaming soup went everywhere
And made a quite appalling mess
Of Mrs. Drury's party dress.
She made a sort of gasping sound
And toppled, fainting, to the ground,
And lay inert by Elsie Toop
Completely soaked in onion soup!

Everybody was aghast…
But then, reacting very fast,
Albert Flood, The village plumber,
(Who'd passed his First Aid Test that
summer)
Administered the Kiss of Life
To Colonel Drury's prostrate wife!

The Colonel roared: "How dare you, Sir!
You scoundrel! Stop molesting her!"
And promptly threw with all his force
A bottle of tomato sauce
At Albert's head… It had no top!
The contents spurted with a PLOP
All over him, and Mrs. Flood
Went mad and screamed: "My God, It's
blood!"

And in a sudden fit of fury
Tried to strangle Colonel Drury!
"BLOOD!" cried Mrs. Valentine,
And rushed to dial 999,
While others, joining in the fray,
Tried pulling Mrs. Flood away

The Harvest Feast became a war,
And plates went crashing to the floor!

Meanwhile, the District Nurse, Miss Cripps
Had ripped a tablecloth in strips
And tried to bandage Albert's head...
(I can't repeat the things he said)
And Lucy thought: "This Harvest Feast
Is warming up, to say the least!"
Soon clanging bells announced the aid
Of Little Wibley's Fire Brigade!
The leader of this gallant band
Ran to the rescue, hose in hand,
But, slipping on a piece of cake,
He turned the hose on by mistake!

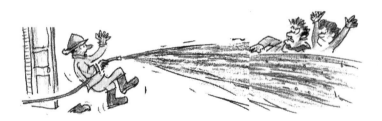

The Vicar prayed, the Colonel swore
As jets of water swept the floor,

And like a salmon, Mrs. Gable
Leapt upon a trestle table…
This flimsy structure, with a groan,
Collapsed beneath her fifteen stone,
And in the wreckage, deathly pale,
She settled like a stranded whale.

Now Lucy, all the time,, sat still,
In safety, on the window sill…
Intrigued, and yet a bit perplexed,
She wondered what would happen next.

A siren wailed above the din,
And P.C. Briggs came running in
But sadly only to collide
With someone trying to get outside,
And as he tumbled, quick as thought,
He grabbed at something for support.

A hundred large balloons at least...
Were thus immediately released...
Red and yellow, blue and green,

They floated down upon a scene
Of total chaos and despair
With soup and trifle every where.
The Colonel now lost all control...
Enraged, he hurled a crusty roll
At P.C. Briggs! It missed... instead
It hit the tuba player's head!
(The band was playing "Stormy Weather"
But now they packed up altogether).
However, this was not the worst,
For BANG! A large balloon then burst...
Like a pistol shot it seemed...
""Don't panic!" Colonel Drury screamed,
"Take cover! Someone's got a gun!"

And seconds later everyone
Had either rushed towards the door

Or flung themselves onto the floor,
And there behind the splintered table,
They lay, along with Mrs. Gable,
Mrs.Drury, Elsie Toop,
And scores of others, soaked in soup
And soggy trifle, orange juice,
Tomato sauce and chocolate mousse!
And Colonel Drury hung his head
And rather wished that he was dead!

The next day, Lucy told her Mum:
"I'm very glad you made me come…
I really liked the Harvest Feast,
It wasn't boring in the least!"

JAMES JAMES

James James
Morrison Morrison-
Ponsonby-Ponsonby-Pryce
Had the
Remarkable habit
Of telling you everything twice!
James James
Morrison Morrison
Must have been weak in the head...
Whenever he met you
In the street
He always always said:
"James James
Thingummy-Thingummy-
Something-or-other am I!
Hallo, hallo! What-ho! What-ho!
Well, well! Goodbye, goodbye!"

LORD WINTERBOTTOM'S INVENTION

The Earl of Sandwich gave his name
To 'sandwiches', his great invention.
He knew that this would bring him fame,
Which, after all, was his intention.
"My name's exactly right!" he said.
"It couldn't be more apt! I mean,
It sounds just like two bits of bread
With something tasty in between!"

Lord Winterbottom, passing by,
Who wanted to invent things too,
Then asked the Earl, "Supposing I
Had thought of it instead of you?"
"You?" said the Earl with great hauteur,
"A name like yours would not be right!
A plate of winterbottoms, Sir,
Would dull the keenest appetite!"

Lord Winterbottom moaned, "Oh dear!
My name's no good for anything!
I'm fond of it, although I fear
It has a cold, posterior ring!"
This set him thinking hard, until
He found the way to fame and riches!
"I know!" he cried at last, "I will
Invent a pair of draughty breeches!"

THE IDLE BEADLE

In the feudal town of Bootle, Mr. Tweedle was the Beadle,
But sadly, Beadle Tweedle was as idle as they come.
The people said, "We're saddled with a Beadle who is addled:
Is our Beadle merely idle? Or is Beadle Tweedle dumb?
No Beadle is entitled just to fiddle and to diddle
And to doodle like a noodle and to dawdle in his bed!
Let us wheedle Beadle Tweedle to be a better Beadle!"
So, the Bootle people went to Beadle Tweedle and they said:

"You're an idle Beadle, Tweedle! You dawdle and you doodle!
You footle round in Bootle in the middle of the day!
Our affairs are in a muddle, yet you paddle in a puddle!
It's a scandal to mishandle Bootle matters in this way!
You yodel like a noodle, singing Polly-Wolly-Doodle,
You fiddle and you twiddle and you waddle like a clown!
But Bootle needs a Beadle who is sharper than a needle,
So stop your fiddle-faddle, or skedaddle...out of town!"

But Beadle Tweedle answered, "Bootle people, I'm
your Beadle!
I'm a model Bootle Beadle and in Bootle I'm the
boss!
If Bootle people meddle with a model Bootle
Beadle
It'll needle Beadle Tweedle and indeed'll make him
cross!
To say you're in a muddle is just fiddle-faddle-
fuddle!
It is total tittle-tattle!" the idle Beadle said.
So the Bootle people knew they couldn't wheedle
Beadle Tweedle,
And they watched the idle Beadle Tweedle toddle
back to bed!

ODE TO TOAD

From my abode
One night I strode
Along a winding country road.
The wind it blowed,
he rain it flowed
But in the dark my torchlight glowed
And soon it showed
A little toad
Asleep in the middle of the road!
Well, I'll be blowed!
What a careless toad...
He should have knowed his Highway Code!

ANITA

Anita was a thoughtful child,
Who loved the creatures of the wild...
Smooth or hairy, large or small,
Plain or striped, she loved them all,
And always had a cheery smile
For any passing crocodile!
(She lived in Africa, you see,
And saw them passing frequently)
But one day it occurred to her
How hungry many of them were!
'It's terrible,' she told her mother,
'I've even seen them eat each other!
Every one of them, I feel,
Would welcome a substantial meal!'
She made her mind up straightaway
To ask them all to tea next day!
The invitation to the feast
Was taken to each bird and beast
By Melchior, her cockatoo,
Who told them what they had to do:
"The party will begin at four!
Come as you are!" said Melchior.
And, otherwise engaged or not,
They all accepted on the spot!
"Tea," exclaimed a porcupine,
"Sends prickles up and down my spine!"
The gnus came first to the repast,
(For gnus can travel very fast)
But soon came antelopes in herds
And flocks of brightly-coloured birds
And crocodiles and chimpanzees
And monkeys swinging through the trees,
And when they came they gasped and said

They'd never witnessed such a spread!
With grunts and roars and yelps and shrieks,
With snuffles and excited squeaks,
To show their heartfelt gratitude,
They fell upon the plates of food!
"Yum-yum!" said one of the baboons,
"I can't resist these macaroons!"
The parrots, with delighted screams,
Attacked the plates of custard creams...
And so, it wasn't long before
No crumb was left, and what is more,
An ostrich saved the washing-up
By swallowing his plate and cup!
"I can't recall," a hippo sighed,
"When I have felt so satisfied!"
And every bird and every beast
Agreed it was a splendid feast.
"The only thing," said one baboon,
"Which rather spoiled the afternoon,
Was when that absent-minded cheetah
Forgot himself and ate * * * * *!

EMILY'S FEMILY

Let's go round to Emily's place,

For Emily's femily's awfly nace!

And if we stay to lunch with them

They'll offer us a slace of hem!

GOOD EVENING, MRS. PERKINS

'Good evening, Mrs. Perkins,
Here's what I suggest…'

'WILL YOU PLEASE BEHAVE YOURSELF'
YOU HORRID LITTLE PEST!'

'I wonder, would you pop around
At six o'clock tonight?'

'YOU WON'T GET ANY SUPPER
AND THAT WILL SERVE YOU RIGHT!'

'Good Heavens, Mrs. Perkins!
What was that you said?'

'DON'T TRY IT ON WITH ME, MY GIRL!'

'Oh dear, the phone's gone dead!'

MY DYPEWRIDER

My dypewrider is very old...
Id lacks one very vidal key,
And consequendly, as you see,
I always subsdidude a 'd'.

I saw id in a jumble sale.
"A dypewrider!" I cried. "Delighdful!"
I needed one because, you see,
My hand-wriding is simply frighdful!

Id only cosd me fifdy p.
Whad a bargain I had god!
I god a drain to ged id home
Because id weighed an awful lod!

Id's nod ideal, I will admid,
Because, apard from being old,
Id makes me sound a liddle bid
As if I've god a sdreaming cold!

THE MOOSE AND THE YAK

The mighty moose
Needs no excuse
To reproduce,
But it seems the yak
Has lost the knack.
That's why the moose
Is so profuse
And the world lacks
Yaks.

SIR SAMSON SIMPSON'S SLOOP
(a poem in which all words begins with the letter S)

Samantha smiled. She stood surveying
Shoreham's shingly, shimmering seashore.
Sweet Samantha! (Strictly speaking
Samantha Seymour-Spencer-Scott!)
Shoreham, Sussex, simply sweltered!
September sunshine seemed so scorching
Sensibly she started strolling,
Seeking some secluded spot!

Such salubrious surroundings
Sent Samantha's spirits soaring!
She saw some skylarks singing sweetly,
Spotted several swallows swoop...
Slowly, sensuously she sauntered,
Savouring Shoreham's scenic splendour...
Soon she sighted 'Salamander',
Sir Samson Simpson's splendid sloop!

Simultaneously, Sir Samson
(Salamander's stalwart skipper)
Sitting sipping Spanish sherry,
Saw Samantha slowly stroll...
She seemed so stunning, so seductive,
Strange sensations seized Sir Samson!
Such superb sophistication
Stirred Sir Samson's simple soul!

Samantha's stylish strapless swimsuit,
(So spectacularly scanty!)
Showing slender suntanned shoulders,
Sir Samson slyly scrutinised.

Suddenly, severely smitten,
Shorewards strode Sir Samson Simpson,
Shouting sharply: 'Stop, Samantha...!'
So, she stopped, somewhat surprised.

Sir Samson straightaway suggested
Sailing Salamander somewhere...
'Sailing's splendid sport, Samantha!'
Slightly sceptical, she stood.
Silently she speculated,
Smiling shyly. Should she spurn
Sir Samson's singular suggestion?
Strictly, she supposed she should!

Still, Sir Samson seemed straightforward,
So, square-shouldered, so substantial!
Surely Shoreham's safest sailor,
Sir Samson Simpson stood supreme!
So, suppressing silly scruples,
She spontaneously submitted:
'Sir,' she said, saluting smartly,
'Super! Simply splendid scheme!'

Speedily Sir Samson started
Stowing ship's supplies securely...
Seamen's sweaters, spare sou'westers,
Scottish shortbread (slightly stale),
Soup, smoked salmon sandwiches, satsumas,
Sherry (specially selected) ...
'She's shipshape, skipper!' said Samantha...
So, Sir Samson's sloop set sail!

Someone, scanning Shoreham's seashore,
Spotted Salamander sailing...
Sir Samson's spinster sister, Sibyl!
Surreptitiously she spied.

Shocked, she saw Sir Samson steering,
Saw Samantha's strapless swimsuit...
'Samson's so supremely stupid,
So susceptible!' she sighed.

Suppose, she surmised, some spectator,
Seeing Salamander sailing
Started spreading spicy stories?
(Stuffy, Shoreham's social scene!)
Sibyl's sour suspicions strengthened...
Secretly she scented scandal!
'Samson's sixty-six!' she spluttered,
'Samantha's scarcely seventeen!'

Swelling sails sent Salamander
Skimming swiftly, smoothly southward...
Scintillating sunshine sparkled,
Superlative, Sir Samson's skill!
Samantha, spellbound, started singing...
Sir Samson, smiling, sipped some sherry...
(Sweet, Sir Samson Simpson's sherry,
Samantha's singing, sweeter still!)

Suddenly Samantha stiffened...
Stormy skies succeeded sunshine,
Salty sea-spray, stinging, splashing,
Soaked Sir Samson's speeding sloop!
Samantha's singing stopped. She shivered...
So, sympathetically, Sir Samson,
Sensing she seemed slightly seasick,
Served some savoury-smelling soup!

'Soup, Samantha,' said Sir Samson,
'Stiffens sinews, settles stomachs!
Soup's so soothing, so sustaining,
Seasick symptoms soon subside!'

So, Samantha, sighing sadly,
Swallowed several steaming spoonfuls.
'Sherry's similarly soothing!'
Said Sir Samson, satisfied.

Sailing soon seemed suicidal...
Stupendous seas struck Salamander!
Samantha's stomach suffered spasms
So severe she scarcely stirred.
Strangely stoical, Sir Samson
Still sat swigging sherry, saying:
'Sip some soothing soup, Samantha!'
Sounding seriously slurred.

Stark, Samantha's situation!
She saw Sir Samson sleeping soundly!
Stormswept, shattered, Salamander
Slowly, sickeningly surged!
Suddenly she shuddered sharply...
Samantha shrieked: 'She's sinking, skipper!'
Sixty seconds subsequently
Sir Samson's stricken sloop submerged!

Spluttering, Samantha surfaced...
Straightaway, she saw Sir Samson
Senseless, speechless, (sadly sloopless),
Stoned! Samantha's stomach shrank!
Shocked, scared stiff, she started screaming:
'Swim, Sir Samson!' Stony silence!
Slowly, sixteen-stone Sir Samson,
Shoreham's safest sailor, sank!

Shortly, some sixth sense suggested
Screaming surely spelt surrender!
Should she spinelessly succumb?
Somehow, she'd survive, she swore!

Such speculations spurred Samantha...
So, since staying still seemed stupid,
Sensibly she started swimming,
Seeking Shoreham's shingly shore.

See Samantha, swimming sidestroke!
Sweating...struggling...striving...straining...
Seeking safety...succour... shelter...
Stoutly, steadfastly, she swims!
(-Scribe! Stop sounding so sententious!
Stylists scorn such sloppy scribbling!
Simplify Samantha's story...
Shun superfluous synonyms!')
....
Surprisingly, successive sea-swells
Swept Samantha slowly shorewards!
Showing superhuman spirit
Somehow, stubbornly, she strived.
Soon, something stony scraped Samantha:
Shoreham's steeply-shelving shingle!
She scrabbled, scrambled...soon stood
swaying...
Stumbled, swooned! So, she survived!

Shoreham's Sunday Sport soon stated:
'STORM SINKS SLOOP! SLOSHED
SKIPPER SCUPPERED!
SCHOOLGIRL SWEETHEART SOLE
SURVIVOR!
SIR SAMSON'S SISTER SCANDALISED!'
Sibyl Simpson, strangely sanguine,
Scorning sympathy, said simply
She'd seldom seen such shameful stories
So succinctly summarised!

Samantha still spends sunny summers
Strolling sadly, staring seaward...
Sometimes still, she swears she sees
Sir Samson's seaweed-shrouded sloop!
Strange, Samantha's superstition!
Stranger still, she sometimes senses
Someone, sounding sozzled, saying:
'Soup, Samantha! Sip some soup!'

FISHING

Bertie	BOUGHT
A fishing	BOAT
And sailed a-	BOUT
For quite a	BIT,
And used the	BAIT
That he had	BROUGHT
Hurray! said	BERT
I've got a	BITE!
It is, I	BET
A hali-	BUT!
But Bert was	BEAT
He caught a	BOOT!

THE CRICKET MATCH

There was one to tie
And two to win
And I knew that I
Was the last man in.
The bowler grinned
When I appeared:
He had two short legs
And a big black beard!
The light was bad
And the pitch was hard
And I shook like mad
As I took my guard.
But my captain's words
Came back to me:
"Let boldness be
Your friend!" said he.
So I felt no sort
Of fear at all:
"Be bold!" I thought…
And I was…. first ball!

FIRST DAY

It was very exciting! I met all the others...
There's Flora and Laura and Nora and Pete
And Shirley Carruthers (who hates both her
brothers)
And Sally O'Malley (who gave me a sweet)
And Stephanie Walker (who's been to
Majorca)
And Benny and Penny and Jonathan Pratt
And Annie and Danny (who lives with his
Granny)
And Ronald MacDonald (who's got a new
cat)
And Eddie and Freddie and James (who
wears glasses)
And Lisa Teresa van Doorn (who is Dutch!)
And Sharon and Karen (who has dancing
classes)
And Albert and Mal but I don't like him
much!
And Tony Malony and Emily Evans
And Jerry and Terry (who cried! What a
shame!)
And Kate who was late and who else? Oh,
good heavens!
I've gone and forgotten Miss Thingummy's
name!

GOOD NEWS AND BAD NEWS

What splendid news! That's great! Hurray!
Well done! But wait! What's that you say?
Oh surely not?! Oh, what a blow.
That's terrible! Oh dear! Oh NO!

THE GREAT BERNARDO

One evening at the Albert Hall
The violinist had a fall.
He groaned: "I've injured something vital!
I'll have to cancel my recital!
Up sprang the Great Bernardo Brown…
"You cannot let the people down!
I'll be the soloist," he said,
"So let the concert go ahead!
Lend me a fiddle and a bow
And I'll be pleased to have a go!"
How brilliantly Bernardo played
Satsuma's B-Flat Serenade!
The twiddly bits were a sensation
And he received a huge ovation!

Above the Channel one dark night
The jumbo jet was losing height…
The starboard engine gave a cough
And died! And then the tail fell off!
The Captain cried: "Well thank the Lord!
The Great Bernardo is on board!
He's the man to get us down!"
And soon the Great Bernardo Brown
Was in control. With icy calm
He soothed the passengers' alarm
And with unprecedented skill
He flew the stricken plane until
He saw the runway lights below
And landed safely at Heathrow!

Her Majesty, at Windsor Castle,
One night was playing 'Pass the Parcel',
With all the Royal Family there

And happy faces everywhere.
Just as it seemed the Queen might win
The Great Bernardo Brown rushed in…
"Give me the parcel, Ma'am!" he cried,
"There is a ticking bomb inside!"
In seconds he removed the fuse
As they stood quaking in their shoes.
"Thank God I was in time!" he said,
"For otherwise you'd all be dead!"
The Queen, as calm as calm could be
Awarded him the OBE!

The nation's leader held his head:
"This country's in a mess," he said.
Inflation's up, investment's down…
I need the Great Bernardo Brown,
For he's the only person who
Can tell me what I ought to do!"
He rang that evening from Whitehall…
Bernardo's mother took the call;
"Hallo, Prime Minister," she said,
"I'm sorry, Bernie's gone to bed.
He can't come round, it's far too late…
Don't forget, he's only eight!
Besides, if I remember right,
He's playing for the Spurs tonight!"

MY LIMERICK

Whenever this rhyme is rehearsed
Line two sounds as bad as the first,
The third line is poor,
And so is line four,
But the last line is always the worst!

WILLIAM

-William, have you done your homework?
　　William, has the cat been fed?
　　Have you washed your face this morning,
　　Cleaned your teeth and made your bed?

-William, it's your mother speaking!
　　Answer when I speak to you!
　　Are you going to sit there watching
　　Television all day through?

-Mother, I will not deceive you...
　　So, I may as well confess,
　　The answers to your many questions
　　Are no, no, no, no and yes!

CREATURES STRANGE AND RARE

The old professor was ninety-three,
And he wagged his beard as he said to me:
"I have spent my life, and lost my hair,
In the study of creatures strange and rare!
Whatever you want to know," he said,
"It's all in here!" and he tapped his head.
I thought: "He's round the bend all right!"
But I asked him, wishing to be polite,
"What is that creature by your side?"
"A Chocolate Moose!" the sage replied.
"I know no animal quite so sweet!"
And he gave it a lump of sugar to eat.
"Of course," he went on, "the Blithering Ass
Is all too common today, alas!
But there's one creature all too rare...
The genuine, golden Long Blonde Hare!
And I love to see, and so would you,
The innocent eyes of a Nearly-Gnu!
How marvellous it is to hear
The mournful sigh of the Dear-O Deer,
Or the high-pitched squeak of the Baseball Bat...
I simply never get tired of that!
Or the sound which echoes across the bay
Of the Whale of Anguish at break of day!
Oh, I have followed for hours and more
The relentless drone of the Crashing Boar
As his thundering hoofs pursued the track
Of the irrepressible Yakkity-Yak!
And many a time I've been in a jam...
Alone, with a furious Battering Ram!
My friend, there's nothing that can compare
With the study of creatures strange and rare!
And now, Good Day to you! Time for bed!"
And a Seal of Approval nodded its head!

MRS. DROOD

Once a year, at Hallowe'en,
Mrs. Drood of Parson's Green
Would walk the streets with measured tread,
A silver saucepan on her head.
When asked the reason, she would say:
'To keep the elephants away!'
The people laughed at Mrs. Drood,
Which was unkind and very rude,
But when they said, 'There's never been
An elephant in Parson's Green!'
She merely smiled and said 'I know!
And I intend to keep it so!'

But then one year, at Hallowe'en,
There was a most unpleasant scene.
A crowd of people came and stood
Outside the house of Mrs. Drood.
They loudly jeered at her and laughed
And made it plain they thought her daft.
'Quick, put your saucepan on!' they cried,
'There's herds of elephants outside!'
Their rudeness and ingratitude
Were just too much for Mrs. Drood...
She took the bus to Ponders End
To spend the evening with a friend.

That night, a dreadful thing occurred...
The sound of trumpeting was heard,
And twenty elephants were seen
Slowly approaching Parson's Green!
What panic elephants can cause!
Everybody locked their doors,
Police appealed in vain for calm,

And someone rang the fire alarm!
The elephants, up-rooting shrubs
And overturning garden tubs,
Came trundling up the New King's Road,
Oblivious of the Highway Code!
They trampled all the garden gnomes
While people trembled in their homes!
But just when things were looking black,
Thank Heavens! Mrs. Drood came back!
Calm and confident, she strode
Down the middle of the road!
Like a knight of old she seemed
And on her head the saucepan gleamed!
It shone with a mysterious light...
Which put the elephants to flight!

Away they lumbered through the night,
Ignoring every traffic light,
Across the bridge, up Putney Hill,
On and on they went until
They disappeared into the dark
And wild terrain of Richmond Park!

In Parson's Green, the sheer relief
Was really quite beyond belief!
Everyone ran out to greet
Their gallant saviour in the street...
A heroine was Mrs. Drood!
They showered her with gratitude,
With gifts of marmalade and plums
And bunches of chrysanthemums
And tickets for the pantomime!
Then, in the very nick of time
Kate Adie came and interviewed
The celebrated Mrs. Drood!
And after that, as you'd expect,
The people showed her great respect.
Since then, no-one has ever seen
An elephant in Parson's Green,
Tho' they are said to wander still
In Hampton Wick and Strawberry Hill!

MY PET

I don't want a pet
Like a marmoset...
And I couldn't cope
With an antelope.
I'd run a mile
From a crocodile,
Nor should I care
For a grizzly bear!
I don't in the least
Want a wildebeest...
Only a puppy
Will make me huppy!

SIR HARPER SWAN

Sir Harper Swan won wide acclaim
As Ireland's foremost poet.
It's strange how he acquired his name…
You'll be surprised to know it!

One stormy night in Donegal
Old Mary Flynn was sleeping
When suddenly she woke because
She heard the sound of weeping.

Outside her cottage door she found
A new-born infant lying…
"He's been abandoned!" Mary cried,
"No wonder he is crying!"

She took him in and cared for him
But no-one came to claim him,
So after several weeks she thought
The time had come to name him.

She kissed him on his button nose
And wrapped her arms around him
And named him HARPER SWAN because
That was the hour she found him!

MONTMORENCY

Let me tell you very briefly
What occurred on Monday morning,
Shortly after seven-thirty,
When my cousin Montmorency,
In his slippers and pyjamas,
Went to fetch his morning paper.
I shall tell the dreadful story,
Tell it truly as it happened,
Adding here and there a detail,
Pausing only for reflection...
This will help to build the tension,
Make the story more exciting!

Let me start at the beginning...
From the moment Montmorency,
(Son of my paternal uncle,
Which is why he was my cousin)
Woke upon that fateful morning,
Ready for the tasks before him,
Ready for the day's adventure,
Working in his fish and chip shop...
You should know that Montmorency
Ran the local fish and chip shop...
This was sited near the station
And was known as 'Monty's Fishbar'.

So, returning to my story...
Down the stairs went Montmorency,
Looking forward to his breakfast,
-This was often eggs and bacon,
Though he sometimes had a kipper...
(He was partial to a kipper!)

Only when he'd had his breakfast,
Only when he'd put the cat out,
Only then did Montmorency
Go to fetch the morning paper!
Was it there, the morning paper?
Was it lying on the doormat,
In its usual position?
No, regrettably it wasn't!
But instead, upon the doormat
Was an object so appalling,
So incredibly horrendous,
That he could have been forgiven
If his self-control had left him,
If his knees had turned to jelly!

But my cousin Montmorency,
Always one to show composure,
Never one to show emotion,
Far from fainting on the carpet,
Stood and gazed upon the object,
And he merely raised his eyebrows,
Merely murmured, "Well I never!"

Here, perhaps, I ought to mention
That my cousin Montmorency
Has extremely bushy eyebrows,
Black and bushy are his eyebrows,
Like some hairy caterpillar
From a distant tropic jungle,
And in fact, it is misleading
To describe them in the plural,
Since the left one and the right one
Meet each other in the middle,
In the middle of his forehead
Without any interruption.

This, according to Miss Dooley,
Montmorency's next-door neighbour,
Meant that he could not be trusted,
Meant that he would steal your teaspoons
If you asked him round for supper...
Which is why she never did so!
Nothing could persuade Miss Dooley
That my cousin Montmorency
Was a man to be respected,
Always scrupulously honest,
Who would never steal her teaspoons,
Never in a month of Sundays!
Yet she clung to her opinion
Like a wombat to its mother!
"Honest people," said Miss Dooley,
"Have a gap between their eyebrows!
Never trust a man whose eyebrows
Join together in the middle!"
Never would Miss Dooley visit
Montmorency's fish and chip shop
(Known to all as Monty's Fishbar,
As I think I may have told you)
For she thought that he would cheat her,
Thought that he would overcharge her,
Give her cod instead of haddock,
All because his bushy eyebrows
Joined together in the middle!

How mistaken was Miss Dooley,
For my cousin, Montmorency
Was a decent sort of fellow,
Always honest as a bishop!

I can picture Montmorency,
Working at this very moment,
Working in his fish and chip shop,

Dipping bits of fish in batter,
While the customers are waiting,
Drooling in anticipation!
Hake and haddock, cod and coley,
Crisp and golden, fried in batter...
Montmorency's fish is famous,
And his chips are never soggy!
I can smell that sweet aroma
Wafting through the open doorway,
And the smell is so enticing
That my nostrils start to quiver
And my mouth begins to water...
Hunger makes my stomach rumble...
Gentle reader, please forgive me,
But I can resist no longer,
Cannot wait a moment longer!
I can do the double journey,
There and back, in twenty minutes,
Maybe less by walking briskly,
Then I shall resume my story,
Then I shall describe the object,
(So appalling, so horrendous)
Which, I hope you will remember,
Lay on Montmorency's doormat,
Causing him to raise his eyebrows,
And to murmur, "Well, I never!"

STANLEY GRIMES

Stanley Grimes was overweight...
He tipped the scales at twelve stone eight...
Far too much, you must agree
For someone only five foot three!
The cause of his excessive size
Was eating steak and kidney pies,
And lots of chips, and juicy steaks,
And far too many gooey cakes.
To see him eating made you feel
His life was one continuous meal...
His figure was completely round
And nowhere could his waist be found!

A crisis came in Stan's affairs...
One day, he could not climb the stairs!
"This is a problem," Stanley said,
"For how am I to get to bed?"
His conscience told him, "Stan, old son!
It's clear that something must be done...
As all the slimming experts stress,
The answer lies in eating less!"

But Stanley said, "It isn't right
To curb a healthy appetite...
No matter what the experts say,
There's got to be another way!"
Then, since he couldn't go to bed,
He had some fish and chips instead!

"I am too heavy," Stanley thought,
Pouring himself a glass of port,
"But, if I were as light as air,
Then I could climb the steepest stair!
It's gravity alone, I'm sure,
That keeps me anchored to the floor!"

Now Stanley had, when so inclined,
A clever and inventive mind...
He used his scientific skills
To make some little yellow pills,
Which would, provided he were right,
Reduce his weight, and make him light.
He did not hesitate a bit...
He chose a pill, and swallowed it!

Oh, what a great uplifting feeling...
He floated up towards the ceiling,
Just like the bubbles in champagne!
And then... he floated down again!
And as he gently touched the floor
He thought his problems were no more.
"I am the first who has defied
The law of gravity!" he cried.

And then, although the hour was late,
He had a snack to celebrate!
"And now for one more pill," he said,
"To help me float upstairs to bed!"
And soon he slept, with pleasant dreams
Of walnut whips and custard creams!

Next morning, Stanley Grimes was seen
Strolling towards the Village Green,
And there a smile lit up his face...
The Village Sports were taking place!
The High Jump was about to start
And he decided to take part.

"I may be overweight," he thought,
"But though I'm not cut out for sport
My yellow pills are Heaven-sent
For this particular event.
The High Jump! That's the thing for me…
I'll go and pay my entry fee!"

A dozen athletes limbered up
Hoping to win the High Jump Cup,
And Stanley thought. "How thin they are!"
And munched another chocolate bar.
He sat and watched. An hour passed…
The other athletes were at last
Eliminated, one by one…
And Stanley hadn't yet begun!
He told the judge: "The bar's too low!
Raise it as high as it will go!"

His chances of success seemed slight
For now the bar was twice his height…
But Stanley didn't give two hoots…
Still wearing his cap and big brown boots
Towards the High Jump bar he clumped,
Swallowed a yellow pill… and jumped!

He floated with consummate ease
Like thistledown upon the breeze
And cleared the bar by several feet!
His yellow pill had worked a treat!
No-one could believe their eyes,
At first they stood in stunned surprise
And then they ran across the track
And cheered and clapped him on the back!
Stanley smiled and said: "How kind!"
With charm and modesty he signed
Some autographs… Then off he went
In search of the refreshment tent!

The news of Stanley's epic jump
Spread far beyond the Village Pump
A photograph of Stanley Grimes
Was published in the Sunday Times,
And many said he was by far
Great Britain's finest High Jump star!

In awe, the Press began to speak
Of Stanley's effortless technique…
And when they asked: "How DO you do it?"
He said that there was nothing to it,
And then amazed them by explaining
He never tired himself by training!

That summer, in the U.S.A.
(In Arizona by the way)
The next Olympic Games were due!
Great Britain's medal hopes were few…
So it was hardly unexpected
That Stanley Grimes should be selected!
The Sporting Press was, to a man,
Predicting victory for Stan,
And people read the headlines bold:
"STAN THE MAN TO GO FOR GOLD!"

When finally the Games began
The talk was all of "Stan the Man"…
With confidence he faced the Press
And was a popular success.
"How's the training going, Stan/?
Asked the Daily Mirror man,
And Stanley said: "With my physique
The training has to be unique…
I'll tell you why I'm fit and strong…
The canteen's open all day long!"

The climax to the games arrived
And only the finalists survived…
The splendid stadium was packed!
The main attraction was in fact
The brightest star of modern times:
The famous athlete Stanley Grimes!
(The heats had been a piece of cake,
One jump was all he'd had to make}.
The High Jump Final now began
With rousing cheers for "Stan the Man".

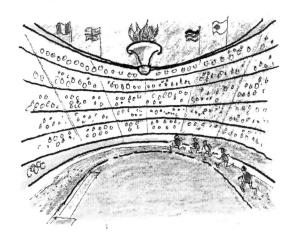

Stan told the judges: "To succeed,
A single jump is all I need.
I'll save my strength and only try
When the bar is REALLY high!"
He sat and licked a large ice-cream
And thought: "How thin my rivals seem.
And how astonished they will be
To lose to someone fat as me!"

The nervous jumpers paced about
And most of them were soon knocked out...
Only the best were now left in:
The great Canadian Talbot Thynne,
The Chinese champion Lee Ping Hi
(Known as the human butterfly)
And, the Russian, Boris Oblinov,
A spring-heeled jack when taking off!

At last the bar was so high
That Talbot , Boris and Lee Ping Hi
All failed three times. So they retired,
Defeated but nonetheless admired.

And now the crowning moment came
For Stan to win undying fame!
Great Britain's most unlikely star
Toddled up towards the bar...
And then, as his excitement grew
He swallowed not ONE pill... but TWO!

Up he sailed! He cleared the bar…
No-one had ever leapt so far,
He rose to an enormous height
And floated slowly out of sight!

The replay on the television
Confirmed the judges' swift decision:
"It is," they said, "our understanding
That any jump implies a landing......
Without a landing, it's a flight!
The rules are clear , and we are right.
He failed to land on the other side
So Grimes must be disqualified!"

The crowd was stunned for it had been
The highest jump the world had seen!
Later on, it was revealed
That Stanly landed in a field
Some twenty miles away, unhurt
But covered in disgrace and dirt,
And so he traveled home forthwith
(Using the alias of Smith.)

Across the world, the tale was told:
"Why Stanley failed to win the Gold!"
The contest ended in a win
(In case you ask) for Talbot Thynne!

So what of Stanley Grimes today?
He's very well, I'm glad to say!
He leads a quiet life because
He's even fatter than he was!
He still makes little yellow pills
And practices his jumping skills,
Because, you will be pleased to hear
He has begun a new career;
He charges people modest fees
For rescuing their cats from trees!

HANG LOOSE, MOTHER GOOSE!

(Nursery Rhymes from olden times
Seem rather meek and mild,
But these, you'll find, have been designed
To suit the modern child.)

Little Bo-Peep has lost her sheep,
She's also lost her collie,
Four cows, a goat,
Her hat and coat,
Her marbles and her brolly!

There was an old woman who lived in a
boot,
She had so many children she went bald as a
 coot!
She smacked them all soundly, without any
qualms
And went for a drink in the Bricklayer's
Arms!

I hate little pussy...
Her claws are like pins!
And if I go near her
She scratches my shins!

Old King Cole ate a very old sole,
And the very old sole was bad!
He called for a bowl,
And bless my soul!
What an upset tum he had!

I had a little nut-case,
He was my son and heir!
He was nutty as his sister...
They were a nutty pair!
The King of Spain's daughter
Came to visit me,
And said "They're like their father,
As nutty as can be!"

Yankee Doodle came to grief
Feeding his piranhas!
Stuck a finger in the tank,
He must have been bananas!

Rosie's are red,
Violet's are blue,
My pyjamas have spots...
And so do you!

Ring-a-ring-a-roses,
A lot of runny noses!
A tissue! A tissue!
Wipe them down!

Pease porridge thick!
Pease porridge yukk!
Pease porridge makes you sick...
Awful muck!

Humpty Dumpty sat and sighed,
Hoping he wouldn't be boiled or fried.
All in a dither, he fell off the shelf...
And now poor Humpty has scrambled
himself!

Little Jack Horner
Sat in the sauna,
Heating himself by the stove.
He smiled when his tum
Went as red a plum,
And said: 'What a nice shade of mauve!'

Hush-a-bye, Baby, in the tree-top!
-No wonder he cries... it's a forty-foot drop!
When the wind blows, the cradle will rock,
-And Baby will then become speechless
with shock!
When the bough breaks, the cradle will fall,
-He'll learn how to fly long before he can
crawl!
Down will come Baby, cradle and all!
-An excellent lesson for babies who bawl!

Girls and boys, come out to play!
The school is burning bright as day!
Leave your lessons and leave your games
And watch the building go up in flames!
Come with a whoop and come with a call,
The fire brigade can't put it out at all!
Come let us dance and go to town...
Three cheers for the boy who burnt it down!

Mary, Mary. white and hairy,
How very large you've grown!
With massive thighs of wondrous size,
And pretty near seventeen stone!

One, two! Three, four, five!
Once I did a backward dive!
Why did I feel a fool?
Because they hadn't filled the pool!

There is an owl who makes us weep,
The more he hoots, the less we sleep!
The less we sleep, the more he hoots...
O that owls were not such noisy brutes!

Little Boy Blue,
Come blow your horn!
As loud as you can
From dusk to dawn!
What a relief
When morning comes
 And Little Boy Blue
 Starts playing his drums!

The man in the wilderness said to me:
"How far away should a bumble be?"
I answered him as I thought wise:
"As far as he can when the butter flies!"

Polly, put the telly on!
Polly, put the telly on!
I think it's Auntie Nelly on
The B.B.C!
Sukie, switch it off again!
Sukie, switch it off again!
It's Rimsky-Korsakov again!
And the bum of the flightle bee!

Georgie-Porgie, potting the blue,
Missed the ball and broke his cue!
The referee was quick to say:
"Georgie-Porgie, five away!"

Oh, the grand old Duke of York,
He had ten thousand pounds,
He spent it all on a trampoline,
And improved by leaps and bounds!
When he was up he was up,
And when he was down he was down,
And when he was only half-way up.
He was mostly up-side down!

Lucy Locket had a pocket,
Kitty Fisher picked it!
There was but a penny in it...
Even so, she nicked it!

Mary had a wooden leg,
She left it in a shop!
So everywhere that Mary went,
The poor girl had to hop!

The lion and the unicorn
Were chatting on the lawn.
The lion said: "Why do you have
One single, pointed horn?"
"The reason," said the unicorn,
"Is obvious, of course...
With two, I'd be an antelope,
With none, I'd be a horse!"

I do not like thee, Dr. Fell,
The reason is, thy armpits smell!
I'll tell thee something else as well...
I do not envy Mrs. Fell!

Old Mother Hubbard went to the cupboard
To fetch her electric heater.
She found a man there
Who was totally bare,
Who said he was reading the meter!

Jack Spratt was hugely fat,
His wife was far from lean..
And so between them both they broke
The Speak-Your-Weight machine!

Goosey Goosey Glenda,
Whither shall I send her?
The Zoo was the place for
This juvenile offender!
There she met an old man
Who answered all my prayers...
He took her by the left leg
And threw her to the bears!

Half a pound of curry-and-rice!
A takeaway for you, Sir!
Halfway through your Vindaloo
POP to the loo, Sir!

Hickety-Pickety, my black hen,
You've gone broody once again!
Lay an egg, you nincompoop,
Or otherwise you're in the soup!

Tom, Tom the piper's son
Thought the bagpipes weren't much fun.
He told his Pop, you'll get the chop
Unless these awful noises stop!

-Baa-baa black sheep,
You haven't any wool!
-No, Sir, I know, Sir,
I do feel a fool!
One day, the farmer
Took a pair of shears
And now I'm just a little sheep
Who's cold and close to tears!

Peter Piper played a prank on pretty Pippa,
Some pickled prawns in Pippa's pocket Peter Piper
put…
But Pippa's Poppa plucked the prawns from Pippa's
pocket
And put a pound of prickly pears down Peter Piper's
pants!

Eeny meeny miney mo!
Sunny, cloudy, rain or snow?
I'm sure the weather experts go
Eeny meeny miney mo!

Hey diddle diddle,
The Dean plays the fiddle,
The Canons are blowing bassoons…
The Deacon's on drums
While the Sacristan strums
And the Bishop is playing the spoons!

There was a little girl
And her father was an Earl
And they lived in a stately home in Norwich.
When she was good
She had steak and kidney pud
But when she was bad she had porwich!

The Queen of Hearts,
She threw some darts
Which hit the Knave of Clubs
We understand she's now been banned
From all the local pubs!

It's raining, it's pouring!
My old man is snoring!
There's nothing to do
And I'm getting the 'flu
And life is incredibly boring!

Jack and Jill went up the hill,
I hardly need remind you...
They met Bo-Peep who'd lost her sheep
And said: "They're right behind you!"

This little pig went to London
And this little pig went to Rome,
This little pig went to Moscow
And this little pig stayed at home,
And this little pig went "OUI, OUI, OUI"
Because he went to Paris!

Simple Simon met a Pieman
In Trafalgar Square.
Said Simple Simon: "Hallo. Pieman!
Are you Tony Blair?"
Said the Pieman to Simple Simon:
"You fool! I'm James Dalrymple!"
"I'll call you Jim," said Simple Simon,
"And you can call me Simple!"

Early to bed and early to rise
Is a motto no burglar would ever advise!

Rub-a-dub-dub! Three men in a pub…
And who do you think they be?
I've a vague idea they were drinking beer
And I think that one was me!

There was a little man and he had a little gun
And he moaned that he wished he was dead,
dead, dead!
"Pray do not take your life," declared his
little wife,
"Go and mow the lawn instead, stead,
stead!"

Ride a cock horse to Banbury Cross
To dine upon turkey with cranberry sauce…
And after plum pudding and mince pies and
chocs
We shall sleep soundly in front of the box"

Pussy-cat, pussy-cat where have you been?
-I've been to see Tiddles at Number Sixteen!
Pussy-cat, pussy-cat what did you there?
-We tore down the curtains and peed on a
chair!

Tweedledum told Tweedledee:
My supper's very late, Sir!
I asked for it at half past three
And now it's half past eight, Sir!"
"Oh, silly me!" said Tweedledee,
"I've overcooked the meat, Sir!"
"Well, never mind," said Tweedledum,
"Let's go and get a pizza!"

There is an old woman
Lives under a hill…
If the moles haven't got her
The ants soon will!

Ding dong bell!
Pussy isn't well!
Shall we call the vet?
Her tummy is upset!
Has she got a pain?
No, she's well again!
But what a naughty pussy-cat
To eat the budgerigar like that!

See-saw, Margery Daw,
Up and down faster and faster!
Into the blue like a rocket she flew
And now both her legs are in plaster!

Little Muss Muffet sat on a tuffet
Weeping and wailing all day…
A gentleman spied her and gave her some
cider
And THAT blew the cobwebs away!

Doctor Foster went to Gloucester Road
By Underground…
It was mighty fine on the Circle Line
And so he went round and round!

LORD GROUCHY

When people pass by
It is usual to say
'Good morning!' 'Hullo!'
'Wotcher cock!' or 'G-day!'
Or 'Nice weather for ducks!'
Or 'How goes it, OK?'
And they will respond
In a similar way.
But Lord Grouchy will give you
A flea in your ear
And shout 'What the blazes
Are YOU doing here!'

When the time comes to go
The polite thing to say
Is 'Tara!' or 'Enjoy!'
Or 'Have a nice day!'
Or 'See you around!'
Or a simple 'Goodbye!'

'We miss you already!'
The people reply.
But Lord Grouchy will give you
A different riposte
And yell at you: 'Hop it!
Buzz off and get lost!'

JOHN MILTON'S PARROT

John Milton's pet parrot
Once met with disaster…
It got sand in its eyes
And went blind as its master.
A cure was essential
Whatever the cost
So Milton sat down
And wrote 'PARROT EYES LOST'.
The poem was seen
By a noted physician
Who treated the parrot
And cured the condition.
And Milton's admirers
Were shortly impressed
By a sequel whose title
No doubt you have guessed.

THE MEANING OF NAMES

What shall we call the baby?
Oh, parents, do beware!
For choosing any infant's name
Requires a lot of care.
Don't merely say "Belinda's sweet!"
Or "Bruce is rather nice!"
But listen while I offer you
The following advice:

Before your little treasure
Arrives upon the scene,
Obtain a Dictionary of Names,
And find out what they mean.

Here are some examples
To which you can refer...
It could make all the difference
In life, to him or her!

HILARY means 'cheerful',
And HELEN will be 'bright',
But DOUGAL means 'a stranger,
Darker than the night'.

CHARLES will grow up 'manly',
ANDREW will as well,
And TABITHA will one day be
A beautiful 'gazelle'!

KENNETH will be 'handsome',
And AMBROSE quite 'divine',
PHILIP will 'love horses',
And PHOEBE's going to 'shine'.

DAVID means 'beloved',
PETER means 'a stone',
But spare a thought for MONICA...
She'll always be 'alone'!

FLORENCE will be 'blooming',
DOLORES 'full of tears',
And ALGERNON will be 'moustached',
(Though not for several years!)

You'd best beware of GERALD,
For he's going to 'wield a spear',
And avoid the name of LINDA,
Which means 'a snake', I fear!

MABEL will be 'lovable',
ARCHIE will be 'bold',
But DOREEN will be 'sullen', so
Don't say you were not told!

BASIL will be 'kingly',
MAGNUS will be 'great'...
The meaning of each name, you see,
Decides its owner's fate.

So, parents, if your little girl
Starts bleating in her sleep...
It's because you called her RACHEL,
For RACHEL means 'a sheep'!

CAUSE AND EFFECT

When Grandma's parrot laid an egg
She slipped and fell and hurt her leg…
(I should explain that this occurred
To Grandma, not the wretched bird)
This happened half an hour ago
And this is what I want to know:
Did Grandma fall and hurt her leg
BECAUSE the parrot laid an egg?
For close observers might have reckoned
The first event had caused the second.
Yet some might surely have suspected
The two events were unconnected,
Because old ladies sometimes fall
For no apparent cause at all.
Or was a sudden shock to blame,
Since Percy was the parrot's name?
It's hard to say, but this debate
Though full of interest, must wait…
I can't think clearly any more
With Grandma groaning on the floor!

SALLY FORTH AND WANDA FARR

Sally Forth and Wanda Farr
Bought an old and battered car.
Said Sally Forth to Wanda Farr:
"Let's travel south to Zanzibar!"
Said Wanda Farr to Sally Forth:
"And after that, we'll travel north!"
"How adventurous we are!"
Said Sally Forth to Wanda Farr.

WHEN THE DOCTOR'S AWAY

-The Surgery is closed today
As Doctor Pilkington's away.
This notice tells you what to do
Whatever may be wrong with you:
      Try scrambled eggs
      For bandy legs
      And shredded wheat
      For swollen feet.
      Curried prawns
      Are good for corns,
      Carrot cake
      For stomach ache
      And Stilton cheese
      For knobbly knees.
      Try Irish stew
      For colds and 'flu,
      Beef Stroganov
      For a ticklish cough
      And pickled onions
      For painful bunions!
As for me, I find roast duck
Cures almost every thing… Good luck!
I'll see you pretty soon, I guess…
Signed Doctor Pilkington. PS
If you're a hypochondriac
Just go away and don't come back!

THE MYSTERY OF ROSIE PROUT

(A poem written to annoy people who say:
Never end a sentence with a preposition)

When Jack went out
With Rosie Prout
He always called for her at seven...
And always Jack
Would take her back
In through the door before eleven.

He came one day
In the usual way
And knocked at the Prout's front door and waited...
But the chain was on!
Yet Rose was gone...
For nobody came and he grew frustrated!

What, thought Jack,
Was the chain to the door
He always took her
In through on for?

Where was Rose
Whose fond Mama
He'd started getting
On with off to?

What on earth
Was Rosie Prout,
The girl he so looked
Up to up to?

Was it this
That Jack had put
The suit he took her
Out in on for?

Was romance
With Rose, whose spell
He was completely
Under over?

If Rosie Prout
Was really out,
Then what was the chain to the Prout's front door,
Which Jack takes Rose,
The girl he goes
Out with back in through on FOR?

GRANDAD'S SCHOOLDAYS

Dear old Grandad is becoming
More forgetful every year,
Yet, when he recalls his schooldays
His memory is crystal clear.
Grandad says: "I still remember
The splendid voice of Barry Tone,
The snaky charms of Anna Conder,
The appetite of Nora Bone!

Dear Olive Branch was so disarming,
Very sweet was Candy Barr,
Every one liked Crispin Oodles
And envied rich Iona Carr!

A greedy chap was Roland Butter,
A reckless lad was Buster Legge!
And how we laughed when Micky Taker
Said Kitty Wake had laid an egg!

Recently I heard the news
That Dinah Sore is dead and gone,
And Minnie Buss has had a breakdown,
But Percy Vere keeps plodding on!
Jackie Tupp now runs a garage,
Owen Cash is in the red,
Phil McCavity's a dentist
But poor old Dicky Hart is dead.

How I live my School Reunions!
Otis Verrey! Jolyon Bright!
At the next one I'll be meeting
My favourite girl, Tamara Knight!"
But though the date was in his diary
On this occasion he forgot…
"I must be getting old!" sighed Granddad,
"Gordon Bennett! Shirley Knott!"

THE PRINCE OF WALES

The Prince of Wales wears braces
Which are red and white and blue
To show he's patriotic
And British through and through.
Besides, the Heir to England's crown
Must stop his trousers falling down.

CHOIR PRACTICE

We are singing a rollocking kind of a song,
(Sing Ho! for a ride in the wind and the rain!)
It's a simple old song but we still get it wrong
So we're ordered to sing it again and again!

The rhythm is that of a galloping horse,
(Sing rumpetty-tumpetty pudding and pie!)
But we're more like a nag who won't finish the
course
Who staggers along and is likely to die!

The choir will be for it unless it improves,
(Sing lumpetty-crumpetty toad-in-the-hole!)
But instead of suggesting the thunder of hooves
We sound like an elephant out of control!

The practice is over, we've come to a stop,
(Sing Ho,Boy! and Slow Boy! and give him some
hay!)
Tomorrow the concert is certain to flop,
So tear up your ticket and throw it away!

HARCOURT BROWN

When Harcourt Brown was twenty-four
He bought a wig and practised law,
And soon became the brightest star
Of all his colleagues at the Bar!
Indeed, no barrister in town
Could be compared with Harcourt Brown!
Immediately he cut a dash
And earned enormous sums of cash!
In no time, Harcourt could afford
To take exotic trips abroad,
To smoke cigars and drink Campari
And drive about in a Ferrari!
However, Harcourt was concerned
Not only with the cash he earned:
It was his aim and his obsession
To reach the top of his profession.
"It is my dream," he used to say,
"To be a High Court Judge one day!"
But would he ever reach the top?
Or would he merely be a flop?
Harcourt worried more and more
What the future held in store.
"If only I could know," said he,
"What my destiny will be!"

Now, one September, Harcourt went
To spend the weekend down in Kent.
He liked the bracing Kentish air
And had a country cottage there.
How fit and well it made him feel
To play a round of golf at Deal!
(Despite his passion for the law
He had a handicap of four!)

As he approached the village green
He saw a captivating scene...
It was, of course, the village fair,
And Madame Zelda would be there!
Surely, she could tell him all
By gazing in her crystal ball!
He stopped by Madame Zelda's tent,
Made up his mind, and in he went!

At first, she did not speak at all,
But stared into her crystal ball.
Then, in a whisper, she began:
"I see a most distinguished man...
He's young and handsome, tall and slim..."
(And Harcourt knew that he was him!)
"I see him walking down the street
As if the world were at his feet!
I see a crowd of people there,
And suddenly they stop and stare...
And now they point at him and jeer...
They're laughing at him! Dear, oh dear!
For now, I see the reason why..."
Here Madame Zelda gave a sigh,
And said, "I really can't go on...
In any case the picture's gone!"
But Harcourt, wishing to know more,
Demanded, "Tell me what you saw!
And what did all the people see
To make them laugh and jeer at me?"
Then Madame Zelda said, "Your fate
Was terrible to contemplate…
I have to tell you, Mr. Brown,
Your trousers suddenly fell down!"

Harcourt Brown was horrified...
"That is preposterous!" he cried,

"What nonsense! I can only think
Your crystal ball is on the blink!"
But Madame Zelda shook her head...
"That is impossible," she said.
"One day, as sure as eggs are eggs,
The world will see your naked legs!
I deeply sympathise with you,
Yet fortitude may bring you through!"
She gave his arm a friendly squeeze,
And smiled and said, "A fiver, please!"

Stunned and shaken, Harcourt went
Away from Madame Zelda's tent.
Her dire prediction, it was clear,
Could spell the end of his career!
Harcourt Brown was numb with shock...
He saw himself a laughing stock,
Humiliated... in disgrace...
Untrousered in a public place!
So, there he stood, with trembling knees,
Knowing the sword of Damocles
Was hanging just above his head
Suspended on a slender thread!
And Harcourt knew that if it fell...
His trousers surely would, as well!

However, men of dash and flair
Do not surrender to despair.
When problems lay in Harcourt's path
He always took a soothing bath,
And soon, amid the foaming bubbles
He lay and pondered on his troubles.
No man, he thought, in his position,
Should meekly cast aside ambition
Because his trousers might fall down...
Or so it seemed to Harcourt Brown.

Then, as he finished his ablutions,
He found the simplest of solutions!
"If anything is cast aside,
T'will be my trousers!" Harcourt cried.

So this most practical of men
Became a nudist there and then!
Of course, no barrister-at-law
Had practised in the nude before.
Yet Harcourt's legal skill was such
It hardly seemed to matter much...
The Lord Chief Justice was inclined
To view it with an open mind,
And said he did not care a fig
Provided Harcourt wore a wig!
Indeed, it could not be denied
That Harcourt looked most dignified...
And who could fail to be impressed
When he displayed his manly chest?

Thus, he became, at forty-three,
Mr. Harcourt Brown Q.C.
And later on, at fifty-four,
He gained what he'd been waiting for,
An honour no-one could begrudge...
Appointment as a High Court Judge!

Harcourt Brown, I'm pleased to say,
Can still be seen in court today,
A paragon of rectitude
Dispensing justice in the nude!
Of course he has no faith at all
In Madame Zelda's crystal ball...
He's cheated fate for thirty years
And will continue, it appears...
For Mr. Justice Harcourt Brown
Has got no trousers to fall down!

THE HIGHWAYMAN

The wind was a torrent of darkness among the gusty
trees,
The moon was a ghostly galleon, the colour of
mouldy cheese,
The road was all pitted with potholes over the
blasted heath,
        And the highwayman came riding...
        Riding, riding...
The highwayman came riding, gritting his poor old
teeth!

His face was as red as a beetroot, the saddle had
made him sore,
The inn was only a mile away, but he knew he
could ride no more,
So, the highwayman dismounted, and he stood and
muttered "Drat!
        I cannot go on riding...
        Riding, riding...
I cannot go on riding, when both my tyres are flat!"

THE POET'S BREAKFAST

William Wordsworth had a friend
With whom he spent a long weekend,
And in the morning he came down
To breakfast in his dressing gown.
Inspired, the poet cried aloud:
"I wandered lonely as a cloud…"
"'Morning, William!" said his host,
"Stop waffling, lad, and have some toast!"

SAMUEL PROCTOR

It's seldom that a healthy lad
Believes that he is going mad...
But this was why young Samuel Proctor
Hurried off to see the doctor.
"Oh, doctor, help me!" pleaded Sam,
"I'm going mad...I know I am!
I've come to you because, you see,
My eyes are playing tricks on me!
It started without any warning
At breakfast-time the other morning:
As I was sitting down to eat
My usual bowl of shredded wheat,
I noticed that my brother Daniel
Had changed into a Cocker Spaniel!
He growled at me, and rushed about
And barked until I let him out!
But even worse, I saw Louise,
My sister, was a Pekinese!
Now everybody that I meet,
At home, at school, or in the street,
Appears to me to be a dog...
And I am in a total fog!
Since having these hallucinations
My parents have become Dalmatians!
No wonder I am going dotty
When Mum and Dad have gone all spotty!
And yesterday my Auntie Molly,
Who's now a sort of Border Collie,
Was awful when she came to tea:
She chased the cat and went for me!
I cannot tell you how it rankles
When aunts attempt to bite your ankles!
My poor old Granny is a Pug...

She lies there, snuffling, on the rug,
And several more of my relations
Are either Boxers or Alsatians!
What shall I do? Today I found
The vicar was a Basset-Hound!
Oh, doctor, understand my plight:
I cannot sleep, for half the night
My father scratches at the door
And whines! He never did before!
Please doctor, I depend on you...
There must be something you can do
To rid me of these apparitions...
I can't go on in these conditions!"
Sam pleaded, but to no avail...
The doctor merely wagged his tail,
And Sam could only mutter, "Cor!
He's changed into a Labrador!"

MARS

Far away in outer space
Is Mars, a calm and peaceful place,
Where no-one's interested in
The colour of a person's skin,
So racial tension is unknown
And tolerance is always shown.
And this is how it's always been
For every Martian's face is green!

THE SCEPTIC

Among the great philosophers
Was one who stood apart:
A seeker after truth was he,
A Frenchman called Descartes.

He studied many learned books,
Which made him think a lot.
One question exercised his mind:
Did he exist? Or not?

Now from such penetrating minds
No secrets can be hid,
And Descartes, after years of thought,
Discovered that he did!

The answer came upon him
Like the bursting of a dam!
In one immortal phrase, he cried:
"I THINK, THEREFORE I AM!"

Then he summoned all the people,
And bid them gather round,
And listen with attention
To the truth that he had found.

"My friends," he said, "You must not think
Existence is a sham!
The power of thought proves otherwise...
I THINK, THEREFORE I AM!"

Then there was great rejoicing
And the people cried "Hurrah!
At last we know that we exist...
We think, therefore we are!"

And some said they had learned a thing
They never knew before,
And some said they'd suspected it,
But hadn't known for sure!

But one old man stood up and said:
"This nonsense don't fool me!
I never think, and never did...
Yet somehow, here I be!"

And then the old man, full of scorn,
Went home and went to bed,
Falling asleep without a thought
Inside his empty head!

Oh, let him be a warning
To sceptics everywhere...
For when he woke next morning,
He simply wasn't there!

LAND OF MARKS AND SPENCER

Land of Marks and Spencer!
Mother, come with me...
We must buy a nightie
Large enough for thee!
Wider still and wider
Does thy figure get...
God, there's not a nightie
Made to fit thee yet!

SUE'S RECITATION

"Miss Penfold! I have learnt a poem!
I think I've got it right!"
"Well then," Miss Penfold said to Sue,
"Stand up, child, and recite!"

"Oh, water, water everywhere,
And all the boards did shrink...
I'm standing on the kitchen chair
For someone's blocked the sink!"

"Susan! Have you gone insane?
Collect your thoughts and try again!"

"My heart leaps up when I behold
A rainbow in the sky!
It's like a huge banana,
And it makes me want to cry!"

"Susan! I'm becoming vexed!
Bananas, child? Whatever next!"

"I remember, I remember,
The house where I was born,
The broken window, peeling paint
And all the curtains torn!"

"Good gracious, Susan! Peeling paint!
It's quite enough to make one faint!"

"Fair daffodils, we weep to see
You growing through the floor...
I could not love thee, dear, so much,
Loved I not Roger Moore!"

"Susan! I can't believe my ears!
You're quite demented, it appears!"

"In Xanadu, did Kubla Khan
Keep Shetland ponies in a barn..."
"ENOUGH!" Miss Penfold gave a scream...
Sue woke, and it was all a dream!

SIR ISAAC NEWTON

One day, Sir Isaac Newton sat
Beneath an apple tree, when SPLAT!
An apple, round and ripe and red
Fell down and bonked him on the head!
"Egad!" he said, "It would be well
To find out why this apple fell.
It might have fallen upwards, but
Instead it landed on my nut!"
He thought and thought 'til Came the Dawn!
His Law of Gravity was born!
And so today we walk around
Secure and safe upon the ground...
Without Sir Isaac's savoir faire
We might be floating in the air!

THE LAST DODO

On the island of Mauritius
In sixteen eighty-one,
There was a ship-wrecked sailor
Who was sitting in the sun.

All at once the sailor saw
A curious-looking bird...
Its beak was large, its wings were small,
Its shape was quite absurd.

The creature was a dodo...
It seemed lonely and depressed.
"Cheer up, my friend!" the sailor cried,
"Come, sit by me and rest!"

The melancholy bird approached
And said: "How very kind!
I should like to tell my story,
If you're sure you wouldn't mind!"

"Indeed," replied the sailor,
"I can spare an hour or two...
For until it's time for supper
I have nothing else to do!"

"My tale is long," the dodo said,
"And sad as sad can be...."
"Your tail is short!" the sailor said,
"Though sad, I must agree!"

"For many, many centuries,"
Went on the mournful bird,
"We lived upon this island,
And nothing much occurred.

We had no great ambitions
And were happy on the whole,
And apart from other dodos
We never saw a soul!

But then one day we saw a sight
We'd never seen before...
Some sailors came in sailing-ships
And landed on the shore.

We simply stood and stared at them,
(How innocent we were!)
We did not know what dreadful things
Would very soon occur!

For suddenly they turned on us
With club and stick and gun,
And some of us they killed for food,
And some they killed for fun.

We could not fly away because
We cannot fly at all!"
(And here the dodo flapped its wings
Which were extremely small).

"Neither could we run away,
For we are much too fat!"
(And here the sailor nodded.
He'd already noticed that!)

"At last the sailors sailed away,
But later, others came...
And when they saw us standing there,
They killed us just the same.

So now you see me all alone,
And utterly bereft...
For of all the many dodos
I'm the only one who's left!"

A tear fell from the dodo's eye
And trickled down its beak.
"Your prospects," said the sailor,
"Appear extremely bleak!

For if, of all the dodos
You're the only one alive,
I cannot see how dodos,
As a species, can survive!"

"But surely," cried the dodo,
"This cannot be the end!"
The sailor merely winked and said:
"I fear it is, my friend!"

The dodo stared in horror,
And again, the sailor winked.
And then he cooked his supper and...
The dodo was extinct!

The gentle, trusting dodo
Is now, alas, no more...
Wiped out by Homo Sapiens
Upon a tropic shore.

And we should all remember
That this dreadful deed was done
On the island of Mauritius
In sixteen eighty-one!

POOR AND CONTENT IS RICH

Lord Edward lives in the stately home
Of a wealthy aristocrat.
Lady Maud has a villa in Rome
And Sir John has a Mayfair flat.
The Honourable Mrs. Felicity ffitch
Has vast estates in Kent,
So why, despite being terribly rich,
Do none of them seem content?
In an Indian slum lives Ahmed Din
In abject poverty ...but
He's over the moon for he's just moved in
To his very own one-room hut!

IF.....

If your arms were twice as long
You'd be a star at basketball,
And you could do your laces up
Without the need to bend at all.

If you could detach your head,
(Which might be rather fun to do!)
Then you could go and have your bath
And watch the television too!

If life was lived two days ahead,
Tomorrow would be yesterday....
Instead of lying ill in bed
Would I feel better, could you say?

THE GREAT AND THE GOOD

It's a wonderful world
For the Great and the Good...
They have power and wealth
Which we never could!
Such privileged lives
Can never be had
By us, who are merely
The Small and the Bad!

THE WOZZA MAN

(This poem should be recited as quickly
 as possible. The record is 14 seconds)

Once there was a Wozza man
Who came to Banga-Bangalore.
There never was a Wozza man
In Banga-Bangalore before.

He always was a Wozza man,
He was a Wozza man because
His father was a Wozza man,
And what a Wozza man he was!

In Banga-Bangalore one day
The Wozza man devised a plan
Which was a wizard wheeze to say
He was a Wozza-Wozza man!

But this was just the start because
The Wozza-Wozza man began
To tell the world he really was
A Wozza-Wozza-Wozza man!

GOOD KING WENCESLAS AND THE PIE

Good King Wenceslas looked out
And thought he must be dreaming:
A pheasant pie did lie without,
Deep and crisp and steaming!
Hungry was the King that night,
And the pangs were cruel...
When this vision came in sight
He'd had nought but gruel.

"Hither, page, and stand by me,
Something good is smelling!
Yonder pheasant pie, can'st see?
Is it not compelling?"

"Sire, it lies a good way hence,
I can see it clearly...
Hov'ring o'er the forest fence,
Acting very queerly!"
"Bring my hat and bring my net,
The one I use for prawning!
Thou and I shall catch it yet,
'Ere tomorrow morning!"

Page and monarch forth they set
Through the wind unpleasant,
Chasing with the prawning net
Fragrant smells of pheasant!

"Sire, the scent is fainter now,
Though the wind blows stronger...
And the pie, I know not how,
I can see no longer!"

"Mark my anger, good my page!
Hast thou lost our quarry?
Thou shalt find thy monarch's rage
Make thee truly sorry!"

In despair they homeward trod,
And the Saint, as hinted,
Uttered words so very odd
They cannot be printed!

Wherefore learn, there is a fly
Always in the ointment:
Ye who chase pies in the sky
Shall find disappointment!

NEW YEAR RESOLUTIONS

Jasper Jupp informed his wife:
"I am resolved to change my life!
From January the First next year
I'm giving up three things, my dear!
I mean to purify my soul
By discipline and self-control.
First of all I shall deny
Myself the joys of D.I.Y.
And second I will die before
I eat fried liver any more…
And last, I won't abuse your mother,
Which means we must avoid each other!
I'm not just doing this for fun…
I mean to keep them, every one.
And now I'd like to know, my dear,
What YOU are giving up, next year!"
"I can't compete," sighed Mrs. Jupp,
"I think I'm simply giving up!"

GRIMLY-BY-THE-SEA

Art thou weary? Art thou lonely?
Hopeless and depressed?/
Art thou ugly, stupid, boring,
Fat and badly dressed?
Then come to Grimly-by the Sea…
Meet lots of people just like thee!

THE GYMNAST'S YEAR

SPRING   upon your trampoline!
SUMMER salts are pure routine!
AUTUMN attic exercises
WINTER   morrow's bouncing prizes!

LATE!

How well did Joe remember
That morning in November,
(That simply awful morning!)
When he woke up tired and yawning,
For a sudden thought had shaken him:
NO-ONE HAD COME TO WAKEN HIM!
And he bellowed like a rhino:
"Help! It's nearly ten to nine-O!
I'll be late for School Assembly!"
And his knees went weak and trembly.
Oh, his panic and alarm as
He leapt out of his pyjamas...
He was panting as he did it, he
Got dressed with great rapidity!
There wasn't time to spare at all
To wash, or brush his hair at all...
It was far too late to forage
For his usual plate of porridge!
In fact, he quickly reckoned
That he couldn't spare a second
Saying goodbye to his mother
Or his father or his brother!
Feeling colder than an icicle
He sprang onto his bicycle
And pedalled off like lightning
At a speed completely fright'ning
And desperately yearning-O
To reach his place of learning-O!
Disaster! At this juncture
His front tyre got a puncture,
So, he left his bike abandoned,
Grabbed his satchel in his hand, and
Off he went on flying feet, as
If pursued by hungry cheetahs!

Was that the school bell ringing?
Could he hear the sound of singing?
Then Assembly was beginning!
As he ran, his head was spinning!
But at last, in trepidation,
He reached his destination
And was badly disconcerted
For the play-ground was deserted,
And he realised his fate:
He was well and truly LATE!
Just then, old Mr. Sandyman,
The caretaker and handyman,
Saw Joe, who looked half-dead to him,
And so, he gently said to him:
"Come back again on Monday, Joe...
The school is closed on Sunday, Joe!"

THE PARTY

I was feeling quite excited
On the day I was invited
To a party at a house in Muswell Hill!
I arrived and wandered in,
But was met by such a din
That very soon I felt extremely ill!

Then a man came up and said:
"Hullo, my name is Fred!
Are you all right? You're looking very queer!"
When I told him I was poorly,
He replied, "Did you say Morley?"
So, I yelled, "NOT MORLEY...POORLY!" in his
ear.

Then he shouted out, "Oh dear!
There is so much noise in here...
You said you're Pawley-Morley, did you not?"
"No, no! Not Pawley-Morley,"
I explained, "NOT MORLEY... POORLY!"
"And your first name?" he enquired. And I said,
"WHAT?"

He said, "Whatnot Morley-Pawley?
How unusual! But surely
That isn't what you said when you began!"
Then his wife came up and said:
"Do introduce me, Fred!
I long to meet this funny little man!"

How embarrassed I became
When I heard him give my name:
"Mr. Morley-Pawley, darling!" shouted Fred.
"What's his Christian name?" she cried...
"It is Whatnot!" he replied,
"Whatnot Morley-Pawley, darling...so he said!"

Then she twittered like a starling,
"Mr. Morley-Pawley-Darling!
I'll call you Whatnot, if I may, for short!
It is time we celebrated, for I'm sure you are related
To the Morley-Pawley-Darlings of Earl's Court!"

I just sighed and shook my head,
And she grew concerned and said:
"Whatnot Morley-Pawley-Darling, are you ill?"
So, I yelled, "I'M CHARLIE SMITH!"
And I left the house forthwith,
And I've never since been back to Muswell Hill!

THE FONG OF THE FINKING FLOOP

A folo failor failed a floop
One funny afternoon...
But like a fool, he failed the floop
While playing the baffoon!

For foon, there came a fudden ftorm:
The floop began to lift...
The failor knew that if he fank,
He would be forely miffed!

"I'm fat upon my floop," he groaned,
"And foaked with falty foam,
When I could be wearing flippers
In my fitting-room at home!"

Flowly, flowly fank the floop...
Oh, what a forry meff!
And fo he blew a whiffle
To fignal 'F.O.F.'

Then, finally the failor flipped
And fell into the fea...
"Farewell, O faithful floop!" he cried,
"I'm fwimming home to tea!"

But at leaft he learnt a leffon
On that funny afternoon:
Never try to fail a floop
While playing the baffoon!

BANANAS!

Good Heavens," said Dad, "I must have gone mad!
I've put salt in my tea! What's the matter with me?"
But Mother just laughed.
"You have always been daft!
You've been nutty," sha said,
"Since the day we were wed!
But it isn't just you,
All the family too
Is delightfully scatty
And balmy and batty!
Take old Uncle Ron,
He has totally gone!
And Aunt Juliana's
Completely bananas!
Granny's gone dotty,
The children are potty,
('Ive always found Julia
VERY peculiar
And dear little Nell
Has a screw loose as well!)
Even the cats
Would appear to be bats!
We're all of us crazy,
(Especially Aunt Daisy)
There isn't a soul
Who is NOT up the pole,
So I don't care a bit
When you act like a twit
And put salt in your tea!
That seems normal to me!
But what does it matter? I'm mad as a hatter,
And everyone's happy as happy can be!"

MARY KEGGS

How sensible are people who
Are glad they look the way they do!
They may possess a double chin
Or be too fat, or else too thin,
Or have enormous feet perhaps,
Or funny ears, or teeth with gaps,
But do they worry? Not a bit!
They smile and make the best of it!
Such a one was Mary Keggs,
Who had immensely hairy legs...
A fact which anyone might think
Would make a young girl's spirits sink!
But did she keep her legs well hidden
From public view? Of course, she didden!
She knew her legs to be unique
And brushed and combed them twice a
week!
Now obviously, she was loth
To shave or lop this undergrowth,
Knowing the resulting stubble
Would cause her endless future trouble...
Besides she knew that legs with bristles
Do not attract admiring whistles!
When people pointed, or were rude
She bore their taunts with fortitude.

One winter, Mary went to stay
With relatives at Whitley Bay,
A chilly place where people freeze
And girls go blue below the knees!
But Mary walked along the coast
And always felt as warm as toast!
Her hairy legs were such a blessing
Because the weather was depressing!
Indeed, as every day grew duller
She longed to see a splash of colour.
An idea entered Mary's head:
"I know what I shall do," she said,
"I'll dye my hairy legs, I think,
In stripes of orange, green and pink!"
And so, she did, and her reaction
Was one of instant satisfaction!
In fact, without exaggeration,
Her legs created a sensation,
And very shortly they were seen
In many a fashion magazine!
In no time, it had reached the stage
When hairy legs were all the rage,
And girls were suddenly appalled
To realise their legs were bald!
They told each other in despair,
"Our legs are quite devoid of hair!
They're smoother than a billiard ball!"
But fashion buyers heard the call
And quickly ordered massive stocks
Of multi-coloured mohair socks
For girls who wished to copy Mary
But were not naturally hairy!
The price of these was pretty steep,
(For mohair socks are never cheap)
But fashion-conscious girls must do
As fashion experts tell them to!

Yet though it kept them in the swing
It wasn't like the real thing...
And that's why many girls today
Are often heard to sigh and say:
"Oh how we envy Mary Keggs
For her immensely hairy legs!"

DEAR DIARY

Monday, March the twenty-third.
Nothing very much occurred.
Woke, crawled out of bed and dressed.
Had a headache, felt depressed.
Raining hard, still dark outside.
Fed the goldfish, (one has died)
Had some cornflakes, broke a plate,
Went to school, the bus was late.
French and Maths. And French AGAIN!
Football cancelled due to rain.
Disgusting lunch. Rehearsed the play.
Forgot my lines again today.
Mother cross when I got back,
Soaked. Forgot my anorak.
The one remaining goldfish dead.
Homework, supper, bath and bed.
Forecast awful, rain still pouring.
Please God, make my life less boring!

THE TIDES

Here's to Ebenezer tied

To Florence, his eternal bride!

Upon the shore, they come and go...

She follows him when he is low!

When she is high, without demur,

He slowly turns and follows her!

Up and down and in and out,

Taking turn and turn about,

It is their job for evermore

Unceasingly to wash the shore!

How tidily they come and go!

How regular are Ebb and Flo

THE CONCERT

First we heard a string quartet and then a harpsichord duet...

The former was an awesome foursome, the latter was a gruesome twosome

GINGER

My cat is known as Ginger
Although he's black and white.
He sleeps all day upon the mat
And only wakes at night.

But sometimes he lies sprawling
On the sofa or the chairs
And it's really quite appalling
How he covers them with hairs!

I knew I ought to scold him
For that's the master's job
So eventually I told him:
"Ginger, you're a slob!

You act as if you own the house,
You're getting far too fat,
You wouldn't recognize a mouse,
You are a STUPID cat!"

He looked at me unblinking
As I berated him,
And then I started thinking
Maybe he's not so dim.

I rush around each morning
Doing all the household chores
While Ginger lies there yawning
Or sharpening his claws.

It's Ginger, I decided
Who is master of this house.
With all his meals provided
Why should he catch a mouse?

Though he's lazier than ever
I now look up to him:
For Ginger's rather clever
And I'm the one who's dim!

TOURISTS

I went to Paris on the train
And walked beside the River Seine
And by the Eiffel Tower I met
A charming man with a baguette.
"Bonjour, mon ami,"I began,
{Je parle en Francais when I can}
"C'est really magnifique ici!
Quel splendid weather aujourd'hui!
Pensez-vous it's going to rain?"
"Nein!" he said, "Auf wiedersehn!"

From Paris I went on to Rome
And straightaway I felt at home.
How friendly the Italians are!
I said to one man in a bar:
"Buongiorno! Ah, che bello day!"
(When in Rome, that's what you say)
"Prego, tell me, dear Signore,
Che hora is it, per favore?"
But my enquiry was in vain...
"Mein Gott!" he cried, "It's YOU again!"

JOIN THE R.A.F.!

Remember, if you feel inclined
To join the British Army,
You will be fed on bacon rind
And bits of old salami!

You also ought to pause before
You join the Royal Navy...
For there they give you liver, raw,
With cold and lumpy gravy!

But if you're fond of pink champagne
And Dover sole and Quiche Lorraine
And Steak Diane and Boeuf en croute
And Tarte aux Fraises and kiwi fruit
And all served by a master chef...
Then you should join the R.A.F.!
(Where breakfast, I have heard it said,
Is always brought to you in bed!)

SIR GEORGE

Once, said Sir George, my life was sunny,
This was a land of milk and honey
And I was young with pots of money...
But now I'm poor it's not so funny,
I've caught a cold, my nose is runny
And I am not a happy bunny!

BOSOMS

Bosoms are peculiar.
They stick out from your chest.
Some are large and some are small,
But medium is best.
Bosoms are for Ladies
But apparently it's true
That sometimes fat old Gentlemen
Develop bosoms too!
When Ladies get their bosoms
How very proud they are,
And they keep their bosoms safely
In a thing they call a bra.
This stops their bosoms wobbling
And getting in the way…
And I saw my mother's bosoms
When she had a bath today!

THE YOUNG OLD MAN

I used to know a young old man
A hundred years ago...
His eyes were blue as emeralds,
His hair was black as snow.
And since he was my closest friend
(Although we never met)
I constantly remember him
Except when I forget.

One sunny night, while pondering
The Mystery of Life,
He wondered: "What's the Answer?"
So he asked his young old wife.
She said: "But what's the Question?
That's the first thing you should ask,
Then to go and find the Answer
Is a Hard yet simple task!"
He cried: "You bald and hairy fool!
Be silent when you speak!
The Question's unimportant...
It's the Answer that I seek!
It may be here, it may be there,
It may be black or white..."
"Well wrap up warmly, dear," she said,
"It's very hot tonight!"

He took the straight and winding road
That leads down to the hills...
The empty fields were full of cows
And dangerous daffodils.
He shouted: "What's the Answer?"
To a cow without a head,
And wept, because he couldn't hear
A single word it said.

At last, in joyful gloom he found
A barn without a roof,
And there he stayed, for when it rained
The barn was waterproof.
How rapidly the time dragged by!
The years turned into weeks
And he sat upon the ceiling
And the tears ran up his cheeks.
His beard grew short, his temper long…
What COULD the Answer be?
Was it Christopher Columbus?
Was it fifty-five BC?
Perhaps the Answer was the Pope,
Or Weston-Super-Mare…
Or was it just a bar of soap,
Triangular and square?
Then one day he discovered
That it was none of these…
The Answer for a young old man
Was: MACARONI CHEESE!

Longing to see his loathsome wife
He eagerly departed,
And since he hurried slowly
He arrived before he started!
The rising sun was setting
Behind him and before
When finally the young old man
Approached his back front door.
There stood his dear demented wife
To welcome him: "Goodbye!"
And soon her ears were full of tears…
(She'd never learned to cry)
"Come in and stay outside, my dear!
You're dry and soaking wet,
And that is something young old men

Should always never get!
How happy and how sad I am!
How fat and thin you've grown!"
He smiled and said: "I dieted
And put on seven stone!
But last things first! I want some tea…
I like it weak and strong…
Please make it now, or later,
Be slow but don't be long!"
"Impossible! At once, my dear!"
His young old wife declared,
"The favourite meal you hate so much
Is ready, unprepared!"
"Come, tell me what it is!" he cried,
But this was just a tease…
He already knew the Answer:
It was MACARONI CHEESE!

"And now I'm tired and full of beans,"
He said with doleful glee,
"It's down the stairs and up to bed
For young old men like me!"
His hideously lovely wife
Soon tucked out of bed,
And then, with tender loving care,
She bashed him on the head!
Now, when I often seldom think
About that young old man,
Who wore his gloves upon his feet
And walked whene'er he ran,
Such simple complicated thoughts
Invade my empty brain,
That, fast awake, I wonder if
I'm madly going sane!

TRIFLE

When Baby is tearful
And fretful and doleful,
Make him some trifle
And give him a bowlful!
A spoonful of trifle
Makes Baby feel cheerful
When Dad gets an eyeful
And Mum gets an earful!

WEBSTER

Phoebe had a spider
Who could run extremely fast,
He lived on cheese and cider
And his appetite was vast!

The more that Phoebe fed him,
The larger he became,
On a piece of string she led him...
And Webster was his name!

She grew a little wary
As Webster's size increased,
For he was huge and hairy...
An ugly-looking beast!

It was hard to keep things going
With a spider so immense,
Yet Webster kept on growing...
And so did the expense!

How could she keep a spider
Who could consume with ease
A dozen quarts of cider
And pounds and pounds of cheese?

The webs that he was spinning
Had strands as thick as rope,
And Phoebe was beginning
To find she couldn't cope.

"Dear Webster," she said sadly,
For she had a heavy heart,
"Try not to feel too badly
But I fear that we must part!"

Then, as she stood beside him,
She told herself: Of course!
In the Derby I shall ride him,
He's as fast as any horse!

However long the course is
I'm sure as eggs are eggs
He can beat the other horses...
He has twice as many legs!

Now, to ride astride a spider
Is very seldom done
So he was a rank outsider
Priced at sixty-six to one.

The people's eyes grew wider
And they said: "For Heaven's sakes!
There's a young girl on a spider
In the Epsom Derby Stakes!"

This unusual mount of Phoebe's
Filled the ladies with dismay,
Some had the heebie-jeebies,
Some fainted clean away.

Soon the horses were assembled,
With Webster, at the start,
No wonder Phoebe trembled......
She could hear her beating heart!

The favourite looked splendid…
He was Rimsky-Korsakov,
Then a sudden hush descended
And the cry went up: "They're off!"

The people roared with laughter
Seeing Webster in the race
For he trailed a long way after
As Rimsky set the pace.

For a moment Phoebe doubted
Her spider's will to win...
"We're last of all!" she shouted,
This is not a training spin!"

But Webster had been waiting
To make his effort late,
And his speed was devastating
As he scuttled down the straight!

With superb acceleration
Showing stamina and strength,
Webster thrilled the nation
As he won by half a length1

Phoebe's giant spider
Was rewarded then and there
With a bucketful of cider
And a massive Camembert!

And quite unprecedented
Was the memorable scene
When Webster was presented
To Her Majesty the Queen!

Said Phoebe, "Now it's over
My joy cannot be hid!
Oh, Webster, we're in clover!
We've won half a million quid!"

Now the Sport of Kings is bracing
But it causes nervous strain,
So they both retired from racing
And went to live in Spain!

....

To Webster's hour of glory
I must add a final word...
For some may think this story
Is fantastic and absurd.

Yet it strengthens a conviction
I have held from early youth,
That very often fiction
Is much stranger than the truth!

BOB AND HARRY

Bob was a delightful boy,
Harry was his twin.
Bob was full of virtue,
Harry full of sin.

Bob was always studying,
But Harry hated school,
Bob could play the clarinet
But Harry played the fool.

Bob went on to study law,
The hardest of careers,
But Harry's sole accomplishment
Was waggling his ears.

There never was a lawyer
Who worked as hard as Bob,
But Harry was too idle
To find himself a job.

Children, will you copy Bob
And work to get ahead,
Or will you be like Harry
And spend your days in bed?

Can you guess which one of them
Became a millionaire?
Yes, Harry won the lottery….
Isn't life unfair!

THREE UNCLES

Uncle Geoff was flattered when
He met some influential men
Who asked him if he'd like to be
A Governor of the BBC.
"I'd rather not," said Uncle Geoff,
"I'm ninety-three and somewhat deaf!"

When they offered Uncle Ben
The chance to read 'The News at Ten'
Suggesting an enormous fee
And afterwards a cup of tea,
He said, "I really must decline…
I always go to bed at nine!"

A letter came for Uncle Claud:
"You've won a holiday abroad,
A fortnight absolutely free
With your partner in Capri!"
Unfortunately, Uncle Claud
Was serving seven years for fraud

THE SCREAM

I heard a scream at six o'clock this morning,
A piercing scream, enough to wake the dead.
It seemed to come from Mrs. Pringle's cottage
And I wondered if she'd fallen out of bed.

And then I thought of all the other reasons
Which would make a poor old lady want to
scream...
Did she think a mouse was nesting on her pillow?
Had she woken from a terrifying dream?

Perhaps an owl came flying through the window
And startled her by pecking at her toes...
Was that a noise inside the bedroom cupboard?
Would the mouse decide to nibble at her nose?

Had she heard mysterious footsteps in the attic?
Did she panic when she couldn't find the light?
Did she think that she might have heard a burglar
Who was downstairs nicking everything in sight?

So I ran across to Mrs. Pringle's cottage,
And she was feeling very well, it seemed...
There wasn't any reason to be worried:
It was Mrs. Pringle's parrot who had screamed!

THE PASSING OF CHARLOTTE RUSSE

Broad is the Bean and Sloe the Gin
As the Queen of Puddings comes gravely in.

"Come, Maids of Honour, and comfort me
With generous jars of juniper juice,
For our sweetest pudding has ceased to be:
We mourn the passing of Charlotte Russe!

"Cover my head with crepe Suzette,
Victoria sponge my fevered brow…
Bring me a quiche Lorraine, my pet,
For Charlotte Russe is history now!

Let the sausage roll on the ground in grief,
Let the raspberry ripple one final time,
Let the rhubarb crumble in disbelief,
As the pineapple rings his mournful chime!"

And soon the news, like a sandwich spread
To the lonely shore where the lobster paced…
"Let us dress the crabs… in black," he said,
For a dear old pudding who's gone to waste!"

Sloe is the Gin and Broad the bean…
But life goes on…God save the Queen!

ALL CREATURES THAT ON EARTH DO DWELL

I cannot claim for the AGOUTI
Intelligence or charm or beauty
For nothing of him has been found
Apart from droppings on the ground.
From these it seems he's like a rabbit,
A creature of nocturnal habit.
No more is known of the AGOUTI,
Except his smell is rather fruity.

The EMU hates the human race.
If you invade the EMU's space
His one idea is to attack
And kill you like a maniac,
And then you fear you've breathed your last…
You can't escape… he runs too fast.
This vicious bird can be undone,
However, if you have a gun.

The OWL has large unblinking eyes
And is reputed to be wise.
He has the most amazing sight
Enabling him to hunt at night.
And yet it's odd that he should choose
To live on bats and voles and shrews…
This diet causes indigestion
Which calls his wisdom into question.

The PANGOLIN is sly and scaly,
A bit like Benjamin Disraeli
In certain ways. But all the same
Lord Beaconsfield, (as he became)
Though devious and highly strung,

Did not possess a two-foot tongue
Or relish eating ants at all
Or roll himself into a ball.

The SLOTH looks like a dopey clown.
He hangs from branches upside down.
He wears a vacant gormless grin
And sloth is his besetting sin.
The other Deadly Sins at least
Do not arouse this dozy beast...
So we should greet him with acclaim
And wish that we could say the same.

The MANDRILL is, beyond dispute
A hideously ugly brute
With piggy eyes and scarlet rear
And most unpleasant to be near.
He hates the sight of human faces,
But don't we all in certain cases?
This makes me think he is perhaps
Related to us human chaps.

The SPONGE enjoys a simple life
Entirely free from sexual strife,
Because, zoologists confirm,
It can produce both eggs and sperm.
How many problems would be solved
If we had similarly evolved...
We'd sit upon the ocean floor
And sex would trouble us no more!

The VULTURE circles overhead
And swoops on anything that's dead.
He takes the bits he can't digest
And uses them to line his nest.
This bald and hideous carnivore

Can live a hundred years or more,
And so, although his meals are grim
His diet must agree with him.

If the WASP did not exist
It's doubtful that he would be missed.
His sting is painful, so beware
At picnics in the open air.
He buzzes round you and you wait
Until he settles on your plate.
Then you can either spare his life
Or squash him with the butter knife.

The BAT, a sort of flying mouse,
Nests in the attic of a house.
A kind of radar guides his wings
And stops him bumping into things,
But when entangled in your hair
It's best to leave him squeaking there,
For he's protected by the law…
(Though why I'm not entirely sure).

SIR WALTER RALEIGH

Sir Walter Raleigh, rightly known
For chivalry towards the Throne,
One afternoon was standing by
When Queen Elizabeth drew nigh.
A muddy puddle lay ahead
So over it Sir Walter spread
His most expensive velvet cloak.
(He always was a thoughtful bloke
And fond of gestures of this kind)…

It never even crossed his mind
How deep the puddle might have been!
What would have happened if the Queen
Had sunk in mud up to her waist?
Sir Walter would have been disgraced
And doubtless after such a shock
She would have sent him to the block!
But no catastrophe occurred...
The Queen passed by without a word,
Delighted that no slimy ooze
Had soiled her dress or spoiled her shoes!

Alas, this action failed to save
Sir Walter from an early grave...
King James the First then came to power
And sent Sir Walter to the Tower
Because he was (as some maintain)
A relic of the previous reign.
And so Sir Walter, sad to say,
Was executed anyway!

NOTE
His name, insists Professor Malley
Should be pronounced Sir Walter Ralley.
Not so, declares Professor Morley,
You ought to say Sir Walter Rorley...
But I agree with Uncle Charlie
And always say Sir Walter Rarley.

CHARLES DE VERE

Charles de Vere was five years old
And always did as he was told,
So when his mother said that he
Was far too young to watch T.V.
He did not make a scene or cry,
But merely asked his mother why.

"Because, my darling child," she said,
Stroking Charles' curly head,
"Sometimes dreadful things are seen
Upon the television screen...
Things no impressionable boy
Can be permitted to enjoy!
It's better that you go to bed
And read some Nursery Rhymes instead!"

So Charles immediately did
Exactly as his mother bid.
He laid aside the T.V. Times
And read a book of Nursery Rhymes.
He started with the farmer's wife
Who, snatching up a carving knife
Pursued three blind and helpless mice
And sliced their tails off in a trice!
He thought this was tremendous fun,
Then eagerly he read the one
About the boy in Ding-dong-bell
Who threw a pussy down a well!
"We've got a cat," thought Charles de Vere,
"I wonder... where's the well round here?
Then reading on, he wondered why
A strange old woman swallowed a fly...
Bat then he chuckled when she tried

To swallow a horse and promptly died!
How he laughed! But all the same
Such Nursery Rhymes seemed rather tame,
And so, like all red-blooded males,
He started reading Fairy Tales!
The stories of the Brothers Grimm
Especially delighted him...
The one about Red Riding Hood
He thought particularly good.
He loved the bit where Grandmama
Gets eaten by a wolf... Ha-ha!
(A woodman later on attacks
The fearsome creature with an axe)!
And idle Jack was splendid too...
For when he chopped the beanstalk through
The giant landed on his head
And ended crash-bang-wallop, dead!
Charles, enchanted by the flood
Of death and injury and blood
Shocked his mother when he said:
"I'll grind your bones to make my bread!

The lure of television pales
Beside such horrifying tales...
The upshot was that Charles de Vere
Became increasingly, I fear,
Depraved and violent and wild...
Like every other normal child!

GOT'NY CHUTNEY, SYDNEY?

Old Professor Watney,
(The Lecturer in Bot'ny)
Went to Sydney's shop in Putney
To buy a jar of chutney.
"Got'ny chutney, Sydney"?
Said old Professor Watney,
"My old lady, Ariadne,
Was wondering if you had'ny
'Cos she likes a dollop of chutney
On her plate of steak and kidney."

"Let's see now," said old Sydney…
Did he have a jar? Or did'ny?
But the people down in Putney
Didn't often ask for chutney,
And it seemed that poor old Sydney
Had clean forgot to get'ny,
So he told Professor Watney:
"Sorry mate, but we aint got'ny!"

So old Professor Watney,
(The Lecturer in Bot'ny)
Went and told old Ariadne
That old Sydney never had'ny
And she had her steak and kidnet
(Poor old girl!) without'ny chutney!

"Blimey," said old Sydney,
"I'm fond of steak and kidney,
But to smother it with chutney…
That is sheer and utter glutt'ny!"

OLD MRS. ARDEN'S GARDEN

Old Mrs. Arden was fond of her garden
But as she got older and older
Her back started aching from hoeing and raking
And soon she had pains in her shoulder.

The stooping and bending were just never-ending,
And so were the pruning and mowing,
So old Mrs. Arden neglected her garden
And the weeds went on busily growing.

Then early one morning, without any warning,
(Still sleeping was old Mrs Arden)
Old Billy came by with his beard and one eye
And he stared at the over-grown garden.

Now a garden that's needing some vigorous
weeding
Will soon be a jungle without it…
So in no time at all he jumped over the wall
And began to do something about it.

He kept on and on till the weeds were all gone,
For old Billy was never defeated…
It took several hours to attend to the flowers
But he worked till the task was completed.

So when old Mrs.Arden looked out at her garden
It wasn't untidy or weedy…
It was totally cleared… It had all disappeared,
For goats are incredibly greedy!

HENRY'S PRAM

Henry was a pensioner,
He had a basement flat,
He lived on Marmite sandwiches
And wore a bobble hat.

The day came when his rent was raised
And he knew without a doubt
There was no way he could pay it
So the landlord kicked him out.

The old man had to clear his flat…
And feeling very sad
He loaded his possessions
On an ancient pram he had.

Pushing the overloaded pram
He walked a mile or two
And then he sat down on a bench
And wondered what to do.

By chance a wealthy man came by
And noticed Henry's pram…
He was a patron of the Arts,
By name Sir Hugo Lamb.

A strange collection met his eye:
A wind-up gramophone,
A kettle and a Bible
And Henry's old trombone,

A row of campaign medals,
A clock, a garden chair,
Some snapshots of a smiling girl
With flowers in her hair,

An atlas and a telescope,
A bust of Bobby Moore,
Wearing a tattered West Ham scarf...
All these Sir Hugo saw.

"This is a major work of art,"
Sir Hugo Lamb decided.
He asked who had created it
And Henry answered: "I did!"

"I want to buy it from you!"
Declared the millionaire...
He offered fifty thousand pounds
And bought it then and there.

Henry's pram is now installed
Among the priceless gems
Of the Gallery of Modern Art
That lies beside the Thames!

It is, for many visitors
The main attraction now.
It stands beside a pile of bricks
And half a pickled cow.

Those who come to see it
Are often moved to tears...
An old man's history is here,
Collected through the years.

Henry now is settled
In a pleasant little flat,
But he still eats Marmite sandwiches
And wears a bobble hat!

THE PEOPLE IN THE PYRENEES

The people in the Pyrenees
Eat marmalade with frozen peas...
And they believe that seven threes
    Are twenty-two!.
They make their homes in hollow trees
And travel everywhere on skis,
And think that macaroni cheese
    Will cure the flu.

They make a living keeping bees
And selling tins of rusty keys...
They go about in dungarees
    And bowler hats.
They're noted for their knobbly knees..
But do not laugh, it makes them sneeze
And rush into their hollow trees
    Like scalded cats!

But if you say politely, "Please,
I'd like to buy some rusty keys!"
Then straightaway they feel at ease...
    They smile and nod.
So never ridicule or tease
The people in the Pyrenees:
You see, to normal folk like these
    It's YOU who's odd!

SPORTING MEMORIES

Athletics meetings in the sun!
The memories come flooding back...
Remember how we used to run...
    That poker school beside the track?

That morning by the high-jump pit,
Do you remember Mary Morley?
Her mighty leap? The height of it...
    When she saw that creepy-crawly!

Whether it was fine or raining
Throughout the football season, Jim
Was so determined, always training...
    Squeak, his mouse, to sing to him!

That trip to Snowden! What a time!
Remember good old Tony Tupper?
How eagerly he used to climb...
    Into bed straight after supper!

At tennis matches, Janet Purvis,
Dressed in white, a sight to see!
How we praised her graceful service...
    Handing round those cups of tea!

The greatest time? Without a doubt
That wrestling match with Lofty Lister!
Remember? We were both knocked out...
    At meeting Lofty's smashing sister!

David Hornsby lives in London.　He has been
writing poems and illustrating them for many years.
'Tom's Bomb' was written for his son Tom when
he was nine.

ACKNOWLEDGEMENT

With gratitude to Toby Freeman without whom this
book would not have been produced.

ISBN: 978-1-387-18180-3

Printed in Great Britain
by Amazon